I Hear America Swinging

Books by Peter De Vries

PETER De VRIES

I Hear America Swinging

Little, Brown and Company

Boston   Toronto

SECOND PRINTING

Part of Chapter 9 originally appeared in *The New Yorker,* and part
of Chapter 14 originally appeared in *The London Sunday Times Magazine,* both in somewhat different form.

LIBRARY OF CONGRESS CATALOGING IN PUBLICATION DATA
De Vries, Peter.
  I hear America swinging.

  I. Title.
PZ3.D4998Iad   [PS3507.E8673]   813'.5'2   75-44099
ISBN 0-316-18200-1

Designed by Susan Windheim

*Published simultaneously in Canada
by Little, Brown & Company (Canada) Limited*
PRINTED IN THE UNITED STATES OF AMERICA

I Hear America Swinging

I hear America swinging,
The carpenter with his wife or the mason's wife, or even the
mason,
The mason's daughter in love with the boy next door, who is
in love with the boy next door to him,
Everyone free, comrades in arms together, freely swinging,
The butcher singing as he wraps the meat diagonally on the
wrapping paper, never straight, always diagonally,
Thinking as he wraps how he will swing with the fair cus-
tomer come nightfall,
The school teacher, also now free and swinging, never
lonely now, none thirsting for love, none a parched virgin ever,
Herself swinging in turn also with the choirmaster, with
him singing as they swing and swinging as they sing,
All free in the great freedom that is to come, that is already
here, I declare it as I celebrate it,
Every man taking unto himself a wife, no matter whose,
Every woman taking unto herself a husband, no matter
whose,

This is my carol, my refrain, the refrain proclaiming none
    shall refrain,
None caring who does what to whom so long as it is done
    free and swinging,
All free, unbound and boundless in the new freedom, none
    stinting himself or another,
In the new freedom that is surely to come, is already here,
The great Freedom, the great Coming.

— WALT WHITMAN

I, too, beneath your moon, almighty Sex,
Go forth at nightfall crying like a cat.

— EDNA ST. VINCENT MILLAY

I HAD JUST BEEN THROUGH HELL AND MUST HAVE LOOKED LIKE death warmed over walking into the saloon, because when I asked the bartender whether they served zombies he said, "Sure, what'll you have?"

Pleasantries aside, though, he was stalling for time in which to conceal his ignorance of how to mix a drink he'd probably heard tell of but never had any call for here in mid-Iowa. I could see that. So the problem was as much one of saving his face as watering mine. Forcing him to a recipe booklet in the presence of onlooking regulars would have meant acute embarrassment, hardly to be assuaged by my reeling off the various rums and liqueur and other liquid matter composing a zombie. I switched my order to an arf-and-arf, suddenly realizing that nursing several scuttles of suds would more prudently anesthetize the grim hours ahead than a sonic boom or two. Not that the change didn't itself entail a little tutelage. The barman protested that this wasn't no British pub of the sort where I had acquired such tastes, let alone their pronunciations. "We don't have all

3

them light and dark beers and ales and whatnot on tap here, you know, friend, with long handles."

"Of course."

I encouraged him to scrounge around in the back recesses of the lower refrigerated supply cabinets and, avoiding agitation and rejecting despair, see if he couldn't scare up a few bottles of light and dark of whatever brands, imported or otherwise. The search proved astonishingly fruitful for darkest Iowa, including a few bottles of Bass's ale and another British import that would do for the porter half.

"Now then. Take a stein and pour it half full of the one and then half of the other," I told him, not unkindly. "That'll leave half a bottle of each left over," he objected. I assured him that in due course I would have a second, and then without a doubt a third and fourth arf-and-arf, that I could be relied on to consume arf-and-arfs at a rate leaving no unpurchased residue in any of the bottles conjured from the bins in question.

"I think he just likes to say arf-and-arf," I heard him comment to another customer. "He sounds like Orphan Annie's dog."

Halfway through my second stein, I could begin to get my recent ordeal into some kind of perspective, blurred admittedly, and therefore amenable to optimism. At the same time, dull anger helped evoke the disdain harbored by youth for superiors easily to be regarded as fossilized — such as the two who had just put me through the mangle.

My doctoral dissertation on "Causes of Divorce in Southeastern Rural Iowa" had just been rejected by the Social Sciences Department of Demeter University. An

4

hour ago I had faced this tribunal consisting of Timken, head of the department, and the second banana, my sponsor, a man named Sisbower. Timken is a pale, epicene sort with thin lips and a smile like a twist of lemon peel.

"This thesis of yours doesn't come off, Bumpers," he'd said straight out. "It's neither a systematic collation of statistics on the subject, with conclusions suitably drawn, which we had in mind when the topic was originally O.K.'d, nor a convincing assemblage of case histories based on interviews with the people behind the statistics. And you have nothing at all on the percentage of farm folk getting out-of-state divorces, thereby missing a chance to get in a little extrapolation on the economic factor. How many of them can *afford* six weeks' residence in Reno, in terms of either money or time off the land, et cetera." He gave the manuscript on the desk before him a fidget or two, while I shifted from ham to ham, like Sweeney in his bath. "And the interviews themselves are chaotically varied as to length and depth — depending, one can't help inferring, on your degree of amusement with the principals, claimant or otherwise. You linger, for example, with affectionate detail over this hog farmer whose wife took to reading sex manuals and then dragged him off to a marriage counselor in whose office their mating was referred to as acts of congress, till" — here Timken adjusted his glasses and read from the work — "'till I don't know whether my five kids are my own or the product of the state legislature.' End quote. Yet the ground for divorce was the wife's adultery, and that is hardly touched on."

"I couldn't get her to talk, or him to shut up."

5

"That is hardly scientific reason for giving him his head," Sisbower interpolated.

"Then your fancy was also obviously taken by this disreputable codger you call Pulley," Timken continued, "describing in voluminous detail the night he was arrested for drunken horseback riding. How do you explain all that?"

"Well, the man's driver's licence had been suspended for ninety days, you see, wasn't even allowed to get aboard a tractor, wandering into neighboring fields and whatnot — ".

"No, no, I mean how do you explain here again the disproportionate space devoted to your narration of that particular nocturne? The wife got the divorce on desertion. What, exactly, was the nature of that desertion?"

"She threw him out of the house."

Here Timken reached his fingertips under his glasses and rubbed his eyeballs till I thought he might be going to gouge them out as a means of never seeing me again, or my disquisition. I was glad to notice Sisbower glancing at his wristwatch. He had a plane to catch. He was flying to a convention of railroad buffs, and had to be "on his horse within the hour," as he put it. "Please go on, Bumpers," Timken said. "Everything is becoming crystal clear. Including why you like a defendant who runs a crossroads hardware store, 'whom I shall therefore call Ed Dohickey.' We are engaged in serious scholarship here, Bumpers!" he cried aloud.

"The point of the Pulley case is the point I try to make throughout the thesis: the gulf between reality and appearance as expressed in the poor correlation between official 'grounds' for divorce and the actual reasons for the deaths of marriages. Now mind you, Pulley's a drunk — which is also recognized as a ground for divorce in Iowa, I mean habitual drunkenness — but the parties between them decide desertion would be a better way to call it quits. So Mrs. Pulley insists he get lost and stay lost for the requisite span of time so the charge can stick. But both of those causes, along with adultery and any number of other things, constitute evidence of that other great grand overall ground for divorce recognized and defined everywhere as 'irremediable breakdown of a marriage with no reasonable likelihood of preservation.' Leading to a lot of so-called no fault divorces. But what does the term mean? Everything — and nothing."

"But the purpose of your thesis was still to draw some conclusions about the causes of divorce in this certain rural slice of Iowa."

"That is my conclusion, sir. That it can't be done, except with a cigarboxful of meaningless digits. That to think it can be scholastically achieved is to harbor a delusion, and to act on it to pursue a will-o'-the-wisp. That these investigations are foredoomed, the result a mare's nest, the stuff we call human nature being finally as incalculable as it is, utterly elusive to our poor attempts at mathematical statistical measurement."

"I see. You want to be given your Ph.D. on the strength of a dissertation that has successfully demonstrated the imbecility of its having been assigned you by your superiors in the first place."

"I wouldn't go so far as to say that, sir, but you do have the sharpest eye for, how shall I put it, the unexpected that lies in ambush for all intellectual endeavor."

7

"Then we may call your voyage an adventure in serendipity."

That was followed by the famous "dry" smile, given with a little extra twist of lemon. A tiny blond mustache abetted a metaphor I drive into the ground without a shred of remorse.

"Not even people living in what we call intimacy have anything like total access to one another's interior, and a good thing it probably is! How do we know what's going on in somebody else's mind?" I said, a knee in Timken's groin, Sisbower's throat caught in my fingers. "That most official grounds for divorce are cooked-up contrivances mutually agreed on by people who are simply sick of each other, they couldn't say why, is further proof of what I'm trying to emphasize. Who was it said there is no such thing as a fact? And even when the two do coincide, I mean the official ground and the actual reason, in the case say of adultery, we open up a whole new keg of nails about *why* adultery was *committed*. That already shows a certain cleavage between two people, a kind of de facto divorce if you will, behind which there may be further and deeper chasms, either examinable or in turn totally incomprehensible, even to the partners themselves. If all the adulterers were laid end to end . . ."

"Yes, Bumpers?"

"They might reach a conclusion we with our finite minds and poor tools — What I'm trying to say, gentlemen, is that divorce is as complicated as marriage, and that is a relationship inconceivably intricate."

"Which a bachelor like myself can be only hopelessly unequipped to understand."

8

Luckily I remembered what a priest had once retorted when I had levelled at him that very suggestion, asking what right a celibate had to sit in judgement on sexual matters. "Those on the sidelines have the best view of the game," I answered Timken, trying to hand him the marbles. "And as children we've both often been in the line of scrimmage, what? And of course I'm not married myself, yet."

Timken grunted in a seemingly placated manner while Sisbower gave a brisk concurring nod, as for a protégé who had scored a point, albeit against himself. But it was clear he wasn't going to bat for me, at least for the thesis as it was. I continued hurriedly in the confusion I had momentarily managed to create:

"You may or may not know it's my ambition to be a marriage counselor myself. Which is why I've taken such a broad spread of courses in both psychology and social studies, including summer work. I have an intense curiosity about an institution said to be on its last legs, and what better profession in which to exercise it? I mean the place to study the automobile is neither the showroom nor the junkyard but the repair garage. It was my very curiosity — which I trust will enable me to practice creditably when the time comes — that lured me up all the byways you deplore as having fatally undermined the unity of my thesis. So I exceeded the permissible rubbernecking into the private lives behind the statistical monolith I was commissioned to erect. I was seduced from formal scholarship into human —"

On my "drama" Timken stifled a yawn while Sisbower shot another glance under his cuff. But I was determined to empty my quiver, and I climbed to my feet to make that plain.

"What makes one marriage tick for life while the main-spring on another goes in six months? What's behind the young people's current assumption that their grandparents must have been crazy to think anything's for keeps? Impermanence is here to stay, gentlemen, rootlessness so firmly embedded —"

"Bumpers," said Sisbower, shifting from ham to ham, like Sweeney in his bath.

"When did it all go sour, and why? The shadow fall? For these questions and so many more a set of courthouse statistics amounts to not a hill of beans."

The "amounts to not" was stuffy and even pompous, but I had no illusions that it could save me. Too, I made the mistake of pausing to get a grip on the lapels of my coat, in the manner of orators and courtroom attorneys about to shoot their perorations, an opening into which Sisbower quickly darted with a summation of his own.

"So we're faced with the fact that your treatise falls between two stools. Neither a statistical study nor an anthology of case histories, but a scholastically uneasy blend of the two. So perhaps if you settled on the one or the other, that is, reworked in its entirety —"

"No. I can't get cranked up over this again, much less emasculate a paper in a slavish devotion to unity," I said, with a "so there" nod that spelled insurrection for them and suicide for me.

The heat of my revolt was more than half the product of resentment with a mentor who should have taken my part rather than betray me with a few weasel words calculated to yes his own superior. Because the lunatic specialization of graduate scholarship had more than once been the subject of ironic comment by Sisbower, who would for example relate behind his hand that a classmate of his named Littlefield had done his doctorate on "Past Participles of Weak Verbs in Pre-Chaucerian Dialects." He had toted them up and been given a chair in another Midwestern university. He was *the* authority on Middle English weak verbs and had written about them for obscure quarterlies to his dying day. In some furious inversion of the same academic principle that had driven him to their mastery, I for my part had vowed never to learn what weak verbs were. Let them go to hell. I would never look into the matter, going so far as to stop my ears at the threat of hearing them defined in my presence. I would carry my ignorance of them to my own grave, wearing it always in a kind of reverse *panache*. But some curvature of the very anger that had kept me from the dictionary made me rush up the library stairs one day and jerk open the Webster's unabridged, to discover that weak verbs — if you're interested — weak verbs — thou shalt not go hence till thou hast paid the last farthing — are those belonging to the conjugation that forms the past tense and participle by adding the suffix "ed" or "d" or "t," as dash-dashed, grate-grated, deal-dealt. Others such as sing and ring can make it on their own without a suffixial goose. Now you know.

All that indignation was now revived and turned on Sisbower, whose suggestion that I thus narrow my own focus seemed to me a Judas Iscariot–like act, the delivery of his protégé into the hands of the lint pickers who could parlay into tenure the consecration to such things as dental suffixes (as they are called by those pledged to their solemnization). I was blazing with rage yet weak as a verb as I now went on: "That is the whole *point* of the opus. This ... dichotomy," grasping at a word that can sometimes save your hide in the academic bog. "This self-cancelling futility of the enterprise."

"And that of all doctorates, no doubt," Timken interjected, "dryly" again. "I happen to know your opinion of graduate research, Bumpers. It has come to my ears." I might add that those ears were of a size and disposition calling to mind the words of the Psalmist, "Though I take the wings of the morning and fly to the uttermost parts of the sea," or however it goes. I thought of the Biblical text then, not unkindly, as I hastened to reassure both my tormenters that graduate work such as theirs by no means fell within the category regarded by me as jejune.

"Your monograph on the three-generation family in desuetude is definitive," I told Timken, "and might I note the thematic relation it bears to my own interest in the progressively more ramshackle state of the *two*-generation family. Or even the *one*. The dyad as such," I said, figuring it would do my cause no harm to throw in the current idiotic term for a married couple. "And Doctor Sisbower's work on drag-stripping as adolescent courage initiation rite, the parallel with certain American Indian tribes. Brilliant! Absolutely brilliant, both of them, and I might even add seminal," I said, knowing I'd hate myself in the morning. "It's just that I realized early on the unlikelihood of myself ever achieving that kind of limpidity, of globular unity. It would have meant falsely simplistic conclusions about the most tangled of human relationships. You know who said, 'No matter whom you marry, when you wake up the next morning you're married to somebody else.'" No scholar likes to admit ignorance of a source — in this case a character in *Guys and Dolls* — so there was a round of prudential mumbles and throat-clearing as I plowed blindly forward with my point. Sensing by now the thesis *was* probably a hodge-podge, I went for broke on those lines. "I deliberately went out on a limb with this, gentlemen," I said, trusting they'd forget I'd just said the reverse, that I had been unwittingly lured from scholarship into rummaging about in people's lives. "Tried to do something — dare I say *avant-garde?* We've had, as you know, anti-poetry, anti-novels, anti-music, anti-art, anti-you-name-it. All part of the contemporary nihilistic climate. All right. Why not," I continued, brazening out the inspiration with which I had been seized, "an anti-thesis?" I drew a long breath and put the accelerator to the floor. "What I have aimed at, if you fellows can overlook the enterprising audacity of youth, is the first thesis of the Absurd."

"Making you the Ionesco of sociology," said Timken.

"You do me too much honor, sir."

⊙⊙⊙

"Another arf-and-arf."

I slid my empty stein across the pool of wet in which the thesis sat, its brown Manila envelope growing soggy. My spirits were beginning to rise, for I had been struck with an idea for trying out my brainstorm in another quarter. Why not submit the manuscript to the English Department as an anti-novel? Once an agricultural college, as its name suggests, Demeter is now a large and bustling university, and a progressive one where graduate degrees are given for creative works such as poetry and fiction, painting and sculpture and musical composition. Timken and Sisbower were by no means typical of that humming academic hive! The English Department especially was as hospitable to the pioneering as to the traditional, in fact more so. As for the novel itself, that's up for grabs today, and I'm not just thinking of La Belle France. We have novels within novels narrated by characters schizophrenically uncertain as to which they inhabit, or by characters who are fugitives from other novels, all espousing a "relative" reality. We have stories told from varying points of view and from single points of view equally replete with contradiction — from each of which the reader is invited to extract his own "truth." I had recently read a novel in the so-called confessional vein which was a pack of lies from a protagonist only at the end unmasked as a mythomaniac, in this case an amorist of uneven prowess exaggerating conquests that may or may not have taken place — the resulting mirage of his character superseding, as a reality, the realities themselves. We have had novels in the form of diaries, letters mailed and unmailed, psychiatric consultations, and fragments of posthumous manuscript left behind for other authors to make head or tail of, and the reader to draw his own conclusions about theirs. Why not a novel in the form of a Ph.D. thesis whose failure to make sense of the data through which it gropes is precisely its artistic *raison d'être,* expressing as it does that ultimate enigma of life that is the proper domain of literature? With perhaps a preface or afterword slyly identifying it as a satire on a certain academic discipline presuming to be one of the exact sciences.

That, as it turned out, is more or less what happened. I was fortunate in Clapham's seminar as my choice of target. He went for my opus wholeheartedly, enrolling me in his select group of twelve on the strength of it. No stickler for the Aristotelian unities to begin with, he professed special momentary glut with beginnings, middles and ends, those neat canal banks within which life itself refuses to be contained, overflowing them constantly. Too, he had a disheveled domestic life, and a consequently keen interest in the subject of divorce, which did my cause no harm. Not that we couldn't both see *The Apple of Discord* needed an awful lot of work, even as anti-fiction. The title on which I lit you'll no doubt recognize as referring to the golden apple thrown by the goddess of discord to the assembled deities, which was in the end claimed by Aphrodite and put to the disastrous uses we know all too well, culminating in the events at Troy. I laid my investigator-narrator's action in Troy, Iowa, which further catered to the present appetite for symbolism.

All that is incidental to the main story. I resorted to the above measures really only as a way of acquiring the title "Doctor Bumpers" through the side door. Because *Apple* did go through as a Ph.D. thesis in English, and net me my degree. Thus I could eventually go on to practice under that name.

Perched there at the bar, I smiled to myself as I mentally revolved details of my strategy, counting my chickens before they were hatched, admittedly, and yet clairvoyantly as it turned out.

I flagged the bartender with an empty stein held aloft.
"Keep the shampoo coming."
"I think you've had enough."
"Why do you say that?"
"You're looking so much better."

MIDDLE CITY, AS ITS NAME SUGGESTS, IS SET IN THE HEART OF Iowa, a bustling meat-packing and industrial metropolis beyond whose smoking perimeters the fabled grain and pasturelands sweep to the horizon. It was there I opened my office, rather closer to the outskirts of town than its center, not only to avoid high rentals but also to be that much nearer the surrounding farms from which instinct told me some clientele might be drawn, in these days of increasing recourse to marriage counselors in all levels of society. That hunch might prove only a lingering by-product of my thesis, a feeling generated for the folk to whom its labors had drawn *me*. We should have to see.

I had friends in Middle City including a few doctors, from whom I hoped for referrals, but for weeks there was little to do but catch up on the latest books and magazines devoted to my chosen field, or play solitaire at my desk while waiting for the telephone to ring or to catch the sound of a footfall on the stair leading to my second-floor quarters. Then suddenly one afternoon I have a spruce woman in her early middle years sitting across from me, deploring her husband's boasted infidelities, his inattention to her, and his grooming, drinking and even feeding habits. As a mealtime companion he left a lot to be desired, to hear her tell it (with or without the exaggeration against which one must remain on guard in all such recitals of grievance).

"I like a man with a hearty appetite too, but he needs an editor," said the husband's razor-tongued wife, a high-school English teacher also characterized by a liberal use of literary allusion. For neither of which traits, you guessed offhand, the husband could have been much of a match. "He drinks beer straight out of the can at dinner — reminding you of that line from Wallace Stevens, about how 'centurions guffaw and beat their shrilling tankards on the table-boards.' Do you know the poem?"

"You make him sound a man with lots of zest and *brio*. Do go on."

"Slices of bread are buttered whole and then eaten *folded over*? A plate of noodles will seem to have been *inhaled*, as though vanishing into a vacuum cleaner. How does he get these other women?"

"Are you so sure he has them? I mean if you have only his own word for it. I once had a case," I said, appropriating one from a magazine I'd just read, "in which the husband only vindictively *pretended* —"

"Look, why don't you come for dinner one day — the mountain won't come here to Mohammed — and see for yourself. I'll fix his favorite, oxtail ragout. I do a very good ragout, if I do say so myself. Well, he picks the vertebrae up with his fingers, don't you know, and *sucks* the marrow out of them? It's like somebody committing sodomy with food. You've got to tell him."

"I'm sorry, but I think that's your job." I didn't want to get mixed up in this. "You with your gift of language —"

"Then come some afternoon when he's not home," she said, lowering, and then raising, her liquid brown eyes in a manner about which there could be little mistake.

"I'm sorry. You're an extremely attractive woman, in her bloom if I may say so, and I'm distressed that — well, you're distressed. But it would be wrong. If I were the principal, say, of your high school, and we were talking across a luncheon table . . . But in this case it would be wrong. I mean in these circumstances. It would be meaningless — and worse."

"Don't you believe in the new sexual freedom?"

"Maybe more than you do. But between two —"

"I mean where have you been? Don't you know there's now a school of therapy — ?"

"I know perfectly well there is now a school of therapy, and maybe not as new as you think either, in which the psychiatrist goes to bed with the patient. That's not necessarily frowned on even by me, but I'm not a psychiatrist. I can recommend one for you, though," I said, and did.

For a few weeks I had just the one case. Then business fell off a little. Then it picked up a little, in the shape of a man about the same age, who at least represented a striking contrast to his predecessor otherwise.

"What I really felt was a sense of guilt and shame for having failed her, all along the line, in every respect, and our marriage as a result," he said, clasping and unclasping his hands in a manner suggesting that of a man washing

19

them ceaselessly in pantomime. "It came to a head the night before last, in a bitter scene. I couldn't stand myself any longer, the way I'd been treating her. I hated my guts. Suddenly, in an overpowering wave of rage with myself, even loathing, in a fit of blind uncontrollable self-hatred, I . . ."

"Yes?"

"I snatched up the teapot and threw it at her."

"Was there tea in it?" I asked the question almost mechanically. I certainly didn't want to get mixed up in *this*.

"Yes."

"What kind?"

"Lapsang souchong."

"No, I mean hot or cold."

"Hot. But she's going to be all right. Thank God." He buried his face in his hands. "But what of me? What's ever to become of me?"

Witnessing this spasm of self-pity with the distaste normally inspired by that emotion, I couldn't help thinking, "What about me? What is ever to become of me? Am I to go on pimping for shrinks?" again passing across the desk a name and address as I did so. "I think Doctor von Flivver may be able to help you. He might be of help in a case such as yours."

That basic question continued to plague me in the days that followed: when would I begin to realize a practice of my own? That is, when would people beat a path to my door for whom I could *do* something, on lines chosen as those within which I might creditably function and conceivably be of help?

Then came the case that blew me out of the doldrums for

good, and blew indeed straight out of the sticks — a word chosen deliberately to remind us all how we malign that important segment of our population. As I hope you'll see while our principal story unfolds.

◉◉◉

It was one muggy morning in midsummer. Perhaps, I thought as I languidly overturned cards in my solitaire hand, there was a seasonal slump in this line of work. Couples trying to save their marriages with separate, or even joint, vacations. Possibly I should have undertaken some other calling altogether, or, having embraced this one, set up shop out East where the institution of matrimony is in a more ramshackle state. These and kindred ruminations were troubling my mind when I heard footsteps mounting the plank stairway, resonant in disrepair, that led to my lair. I hastily swept the cards into a drawer of my desk and plucked my coat from a rack. The footsteps slowed as a shadow appeared on the opaque pane of my office door. The door opened slowly, and a woman's face appeared around the edge of it, smiling expectantly, almost with a playful tension, as though I had been "found" in a game of hide-and-seek. I thought she might be going to say, "Peek-a-boo."

"Doctor Bumpers?"

"Yes. Won't you come in."

"Thank you."

The caller was in early midlife, with a round face and pink cheeks radiating a general air of robust good health. She was wearing a brown checked coat and a straw bonnet moored into place with a hatpin of the kind I had never

21

expected to see again. She clutched a brown leather bag by
the strap, in a way you associate with women occupying
the cornier levels of lower-middle-class life. This identification had no more than been made, on a sort of sub-cerebral
level, than it was dissolved in confusion by a glimpse of a
Scott Fitzgerald sweatshirt lurking under the houndstooth
coat. Proving again that such forms of social anthropology
are tricky things at best to dabble in. A tweed skirt of
oatmeal weave and green sneakers completed the getup
that sent my presumptions reeling.

"Won't you sit down, Mrs. . . . ?"

"Thank you."

She took the leather armchair reserved for clients while I
got set in my swivel chair to listen. As she settled into her
narrative, I caught myself putting the tips of my fingers
together, no doubt from insecurity.

She described herself as a housewife living near town on
a couple of hundred good acres with a farmer who had
recently, and quite suddenly, "gone into a new phase," the
way "middle-aged men often do," as a result of which they
were "drifting apart." These were all marital-trouble
clichés that might accurately couch the truth, or might
have been picked up by the farmer's wife from magazine
articles, or from my fellow practitioners operating on the
television, now seized on as the handiest means to begin
the ventilation of difficulties she herself didn't quite understand. After about ten minutes of such exposition, she became aware that I was helplessly mesmerized by the Scott
Fitzgerald sweatshirt.

"*That's* part of this new life-style he's adopted, that I'm
talking about, you see. From this fast crowd he's been

going around with in town. He brings them home," she explained.

"The people? From the fast crowd?"

"No, the sweatshirts and T-shirts. He has quite a collection."

"What are some others?" I couldn't help asking.

She looked up at the ceiling. "Oh, Hemingway, Alice B. Toklas, somebody named Cocteau. A foreigner I believe. People like that. Not that we don't all wear them. I find them quite comfortable working around the house, or pitching in out in the field, as I have to do more and more now that he —" She broke off abruptly and asked, "Do you make house calls, Doctor Bumpers?"

I hesitated, baffled by the unexpected question. "I'm not sure I quite understand what you mean. I'm not a medical doctor, you know, my degree is purely academic," I said, laughing oddly for some reason.

"The best way for you to understand what a home-pattern mess we're in is to see it for yourself." Home-pattern. Could it be *she* who had entered a new phase, a housewife in a jargon-launched flight from the tedium of agricultural reality? One who had decided to brighten a humdrum existence with a crisis or two? My curiosity was now quite keen. "I was just thinking — do you happen to be busy for the next couple of hours?"

I pursed my lips dubiously as I tipped forward to consult an appointment calendar destitute of entries. "It so happens I . . . And lunch isn't all that . . . Yes, I might manage a visit. Certainly, if it's what you'd like, Mrs. . . . ."

"Brown."

Thus it was I found myself in a pickup truck speeding

along a dirt road out into open country. The woman filled me in further on the story as we went. It dispelled all speculation that she was trying to lend some drama to her life by making a case history out of it, and served me fair warning that I must not make one of her either . . . yet.

It seemed that Herkimer Brown, whose friends all called him Heck, had been a pious and hard-working farmer who tilled his fields and read his Bible daily, as God's word. Until one day he fell among worldly and high-living companions in town who told him the Bible was simply another book, to be read as literature, just as full of passages to be skipped as of others to be relished and reread. This bunch, all of whom had coffee later instead of with the meal, broadened his horizons further by recommending other things for him to read as well. Still, the parts of the Bible that survived this purge remained among his favorites, the Gospels, for instance, getting better word-of-mouth from him than from almost anyone in that area, as examples of the narrative art at its best. That was about it. The same went for Ecclesiastes, for sheer aphoristic style. "It is right pithy," Mrs. Brown allowed, as we bounced along. She suddenly swerved off the road through an open gate into a wide barnyard. She switched the engine off and surveyed the scene sharply a moment. Then, apparently glimpsing something that had not yet caught my eye, she said, "Swell. You've come at a good time. Follow me," and led the way up the porch steps into the kitchen. There I was told to relax and "get an earful" of the scene that would now ensue.

The farmer was, by chance, browsing through the Bible as he sat under a tree in the back yard, sipping his noonday vermouth cassis, which he fancied with a twist of lime. I was told all this by the wife, who then beckoned me over to the screen door to listen. The tree trunk against which he leaned so obscured my view of him that all I could see was one shoulder and his forelegs.

"You dipping into Ecclesiastes again, I suppose?" she called out.

"Yes," he said. "It's one of those gems you never tire of. You can go back to it again and again. Like *Gatsby* and 'Prufrock,' and parts of *Bank Dick*. I've told you that a hundred times."

The wife gave me a look of interrogation, which I returned with a nod to indicate that I was getting the entire situation in a nutshell. I signed for her to continue.

"Dipping into the Bible just doesn't seem right," she resumed. "You must know that in your heart of hearts. Is this the Bible *Belt*? We always used to read it straight through from beginning to end, families like ours, a chapter each night at supper, and when we finished we'd start all over again with Genesis."

"Which is itself like a month in the country."

"When we also had coffee with the meal," she added pointedly, "instead of later." I was to see that this detail of life-style had somehow got itself firmly fixed in her mind, as a touchstone cleanly dividing social levels: the hard-working from the lollygaggers among whom he had fallen. "We've got to have a talk."

"Perhaps we can have dinner one day soon."

"How about tonight?"

The farmer rose and, after knocking back the last of the vermouth cassis and firing the ice cubes into the grass, told her not to expect him for dinner that evening as he and some of the bunch in town were going to grab an early bite and then catch the first showing at a movie house where they were having a Buster Keaton Festival that week. As he came toward the house I saw that he was wearing an e.e. cummings T-shirt over tan corduroy trousers. For the moment, he thought he would take a snooze.

"Shouldn't you be dusting the crops?" the wife asked, pushing me out of sight for one last moment that I might hear this unobserved.

"Oh, the maid will dust them," the farmer said, and gave his "new" laugh. They hadn't a maid, of course, it was just the way he talked lately.

The wife again looked at me to satisfy herself that I was taking this all in, quite understood her cross. I made clear with a sympathetic sigh that I did, while mentally warning myself against getting mixed up in this case. The wife now signalled her belief that it was best my presence be revealed.

"This is Doctor Bumpers," she said as I emerged from half-hiding in the window corner. "I mentioned I might go see him. He's one of those, you know, marriage counselors?"

"Ah, yes, those ambulance drivers in the war between the sexes," the farmer said, amiably pumping my hand. His grip was firm, and his gaze steady as he sized me up with bright blue eyes set deep in a narrow face with the kind of weathered good looks one could believe came from long exposure to the elements. "Can I offer you something? Plenty of beer here," he went on, opening the refrigerator. "There's a Heineken back there, and oh, I see some Michelob. The two beers to have when you're having more than two," he sang, again giving his "new" laugh.

"I thought we might drop in on those new neighbors down the road tonight," the wife said. "I understand they're very cultured. Antique lovers."

"Yes, I hear they're so antique I very much doubt they're lovers any longer. And I do wish you'd stop talking about dropping in on people, my dear. It's no longer done, and it makes you sound as though you got around by parachute. Well, nice meeting you, Bumpers. Hope we'll see some more of you around. Meanwhile, regards to the Medical Corps."

"My mother might drop — pop in."

"Ah, then our Bumpers has a treat in store. A woman of singular piety, Bumpers, whose birth gem is the brimstone, as you'll see. I'd lay you odds on how long it takes her to get around to quoting Jeremiah. You know, the Prince of Wails."

"God will forgive you, Heck," Mrs. Brown said. "Though what would you say if a bolt of lightning hit you instead?"

"I would say that lightning struck me as a rather unimaginative measure. Well, toodle-oo, Bumpers." And he went on upstairs for the forty winks prescribed as necessary for the social rigors that lay ahead.

"I'm afraid I can't possibly take this case," I told the wife. "I simply wouldn't know where to —"

"Ah, good. There's my mother now." She was peering out the window, holding a chintz curtain aside. "We're in luck. You'll find talking to her very helpful. There are no flies on her, and as the mother-in-law she's had this buster's number from the beginning." She jerked her head toward the ceiling as I stepped to the screen door.

I saw a station wagon bounce to a stop in the yard and the late Edna May Oliver spring out, wearing a large-visored bonnet and half specs, a basket slung on one arm. She came rapidly up the stairs, and as she did so the *New Yorker* T-shirt made me wonder whether the third mutation at which I had been set blinking in the space of an hour mightn't be the mythical but famous Old Lady from Dubuque, come full circle to compatibility with the magazine that had been distinctly not founded for her.

The sartorial schizophrenia was easily and speedily explained. The poke bonnet and granny glasses were an act — but an honest one. A business gimmick based on a trademark. Long a widow, she had supported herself by marketing commercially a line of home-style kitchen products reflecting in every way a cottage cook's perfection. Her potato bread was sheer mouth-watering nostalgia, as I was to find out. Her pickles and relishes were second to none. These had been sold door-to-door for years. What had now suddenly made her business boom store-to-store was an old recipe for tomato cocktail juice evolved, with the aid of herbs and condiments of which the secret was closely guarded, into Mother Sigafoos's Bloody Mary Mix. Her picture appeared on all her product labels, re-enforced by her regular appearances in the same getup in the corner groceries — and now liquor stores — among which she plied her rounds.

"Pleased to meet you," she said when introduced, shaking my hand. "Whew! I like to never got this batch done. I brought you some of these." The basket set on the table contained one each of the aforementioned, and nothing would do but that the guest sample each, at a lunch to consist of ham-and-cheese sandwiches on the potato bread, with bread and butter pickles, and a Bloody Mary made with the mix.

"It's not one of my drinks," I protested, "but I will have a Virgin Mary. That would show your mix off to even better advantage, I mean than with vodka in it."

Mrs. Sigafoos's eyes narrowed as she unbuttoned the bow at her chin and removed the bonnet. "Virgin Mary?" I explained that was a Bloody Mary without the alcohol. "I'm not sure I like that."

"Well then maybe I will have a Bloody Mary."

As she unscrewed the cap from a bottle, while the wife bustled about preparing lunch, she said, "You look from out East." Overriding the explanation that I was a native son merely in part educated there, she went on, "Go to the Algonquin and such. See a lot of celebrities eating dinner in person. You ever hear the one about Benchley and the waiter? Well, Benchley was putting away the sauce, early in the day just like you, at a rate that made the waiter finally say, 'Mr. Benchley, that stuff is slow death.' And Benchley says, 'I'm in no hurry.'" She shook her head, cracking up at the memory. "That Benchley."

There was something odd here. This was certainly not the woman for which Heck had just prepared me. Or was it another side of her, living in paradoxical harmony with the pious part, one it amused him to exaggerate?

Suitable cocktail paraphernalia being guaranteed by the farmer's current urbanization, three Bloody Marys were soon whipped up, for the women were joining me. We clinked glasses, and then as I sipped I was aware of Mother Sigafoos watching me like a hawk with her little lime-green eyes, as though breathlessly hanging on the verdict of a connoisseur. My declared indifference to Bloody Marys seemed forgotten, or beside the point. Maybe it was a tasting ritual in which I, rather than the drink, was being put to the test. I worked my lips appreciatively, nodding approval.

"My God, this is terrific," I said. "It really is. What gives it that extra little . . . extra . . ."

"*Je ne sais quoi?*" she suggested helpfully, leaning across the table.

"Yes. With that . . ."

"Subtle affinity with vodka?" she prompted further, surely quoting from promotional matter that had been drafted for her, or from what somebody had been heard remarking, or both. She settled back. "Ah, that nobody will ever find out. Hattie here don't even know the secret ingredient. I make each batch behind locked doors and drawn shades. Ma Godolphin has been trying to steal my formula for months. That's one of mine enemies in the presence of whom the Lord has prepared a table before me."

"But aren't you required by law to list the ingredients?"

" 'Spices' satisfies the law. Nobody knows which ones. Is it a pinch of chervil or basil, or both together?" she taunted. "A dab of Rosemary, a touch of life everlasting? They'd give their eyeteeth to know, you can bet your boots and save your socks for Sunday. But it's a secret I'll take to my grave. Not very soon I hope." She heaved a long, transitional sigh. "What's with David Niven?"

Mrs. Brown closed the door leading to the rest of the house. "Let's all sit down to our lunch and we can begin our conference. Now then, here's the dope to date."

It was not so much my taking the case as being taken by it. My absorption swiftened greatly with the injection of Mother Sigafoos into the picture. I was determined from the outset to view myself strictly as a family friend, rather than clinician; but that distinction rapidly blurred in the conversation that followed, the purpose of which was to fill Mrs. Sigafoos in on last-minute developments including those to which I had just been privy. We were dealt napkins with sayings on them from a set the wife had won in an elocution contest long ago. Glancing furtively down at mine as I spread it open on my lap, I saw that it read: "Today is the tomorrow you worried about yesterday."

In trying to identify the precise wavelength onto which the farmer had shifted, the wife gave a few recent bulletins, so to speak, on this "other language" he was now talking, beginning with the airy rejoinder just a few moments ago about the maid dusting the crops. The older woman had once worked part-time for a catering service retained by many of the homes the farmer was now in and out of, and as such had a first-hand knowledge of the sort of thing that was rubbing off on him.

"Can you think of some others?" she asked. "That he's said."

"Well, he keeps letting the hired man and me do more and more of the chores, and the other day I asked him why he didn't milk the cows any more, and he says he's avoiding the reeking herd, like Edna St. Vincent Millay tells us to."

"Oh, he's wrong there," I interjected, "quite wrong.

That's Elinor Wylie, if memory serves. But I'll check into it."

"That would be a great help. We've got to start somewhere."

The samples adduced had all seemed to me simple conventional smart talk, but the mother wanted to pin it down still more precisely, as a subspecies the social diagnostician in her thought she had identified, but concerning which she would like a little more evidence. So she said again, "Anything else? I think I know what it is we're up against with our gazebo, but I'd like a few more for-instances."

"Well, let's see," the wife said. "Oh. The other night I mentioned a new movie I'd like to catch at the Bijou III, and he says, 'Oh, I understand it's for the entire family, so it can hardly be for anyone else.' For another, now, paradox like he talks twenty to the dozen lately, he got in at two A.M. after a night out with Ma Godolphin and the bunch, declaring he'd had a ball. So I says I figured he'd been at the dance over to the Grange, and he says good God no, you can't have a ball at a dance, not really, in fact it's the last place. And give his inner-city laugh."

The older woman nodded, setting her cup down. "It's what they call brittle dialogue. It's everywhere. One round of passing the canopies at one of Ma Peckinpaugh's cocktail parties and I can get an earful of it. There's no mistaking it. It's come from the East," she said with an accusatory glance in my direction, "and is working its way steadily West, just like the Rocky Mountain tick coming the other way. Wouldn't you say that, Doctor Bumpers?"

"I think that's undoubtedly what it is," I answered, feeling rather a man of science collaborating on the successful identification of a bacillus. "There's a lot in what you say, Mrs. Sigafoos."

"Couldn't it be just changing styles in humor?" the wife asked, no doubt trying to look on the bright side. "For instance, men used to say, oh, 'I'm not afraid of work. I'll go to sleep alongside of it any time.' What's the difference between that and 'Let the maid dust the crops,' being as how neither of them means it anyway?"

"I think there's a difference," the older woman replied, frowning thoughtfully into her cup. "They *did* their work, is the thing. They didn't knock the work ethic they call it now days. They didn't gallivant; lollygag; fornicate; blaspheme; snooze. They didn't tell you 'Have a nice weekend,' being as how it was Wednesday. Do you agree, Doctor Bumpers?"

"I agree absolutely," I said. And how could one disagree with so redoubtable an analyst of the passing scene? Until such time as more data had been examined, more "feel" of the family pattern here been obtained, one's speech must be "Yea, yea," and "Nay, nay," as enjoined in those Scriptures on which she turned out to be as formidable an authority as Heck had warned. Her late husband had been a minister, whose chapter-and-verse familiarity had rubbed off on her. That I learned in the course of the lift she gave me back to town, where she happened to be headed on her appointed business rounds — for which she again donned the poke bonnet, not neglecting to cover the *New Yorker* T-shirt under a long coat she'd had ready in the station wagon. The stops I had to wait for her to make were small price to pay for the stimulations and enlightenments of that journey.

33

"The Bible is an amazing authority on practically anything," she said, springing in behind the wheel again after making a delivery at a wayside grocery of the kind now called superettes. "Even such a thing as wife swapping was foretold as long ago as the Old Testament, did you know that, Doctor Bumpers? You know where wife swapping — or mixed doubles as Twinkletoes back there calls it — was prophesied in Holy Writ?"

We had to stop almost immediately for a red light at a crossroads, and as we paused I saw a car pass in front of us from an intersecting direction, driven by a woman with the most startling resemblance to my companion. It was no doubt mainly the similarity in rustic dress, but as she shot across our bow I gave my head a shake, thinking I was seeing things.

"Ma Tinklehoff. Home-made tartare sauce. Nobody knows what her secret is, but it's no secret *she's* a tartar."

"Where is wife swapping prophesied in the Old Testament?"

"Jeremiah. Passage where he speaks of men as 'fed horses in the morning, every one neighing after his neighbor's wife.'"

I turned that text over rather dubiously in my mind. There seemed at least an even chance that the Prophet was deploring — or more likely quoting Jehovah as deploring — a state of affairs existing in those times rather than foretelling it of our own, on which perhaps too much is being pinned. However, my knowledge of the Old Testament, and certainly my grasp of the Lamentations, was too flimsy for me to risk taking up the cudgels with my exegetist on the point. Besides, I saw bearing down on me a hallucination twice what Ma Tinklehoff had been.

Mrs. Sigafoos and I *both* seemed to be approaching ourselves at high speed, the only difference being that the youth was behind the wheel in the mirror image, while the woman in the poke bonnet and octagonal specs sat beside him in the passenger's seat.

"Ma Godolphin. Bitch," Mrs. Sigafoos said as we streaked past one another.

The countryside was apparently overrun with "Ma's," each tougher than the last as she did her thing with home-style foodstuffs, cut-throating, price-gouging, driving out of business and being driven, buying each other out and taking each other over. Ma Godolphin was far in the lead in the battle royal, gobbling up the smaller fish into what had become a swelling conglomerate — now in fact operating on a national scale. Not content with a profitable canning and baking concern, she had begun buying up all the farmland she could find for sale as well, so that, supplying her own produce for an ever-expanding line of items, she was on her way to becoming a vertical monopoly in the county. She was the indisputable dynamo among women who themselves all quite lustily exemplified the new emerging feminine self-realization.

"I give her credit," my informant said. "Probably out scouting up acreage right now with one of her henchmen. She'd like to gobble me up, wouldn't she just! I've got a nice little product mix, and she'd give her eyeteeth to have thought of my name — Land's Sakes Brands. Yes, I give her credit. Popping with ideas, and she *lives.* Local queen,

I don't deny it, or that I envy it in a way. All the latest Paris perfumes. You can smell them subtle scents a mile off."

She fell silent. Then stealing a glance in her direction under the pretense of taking in the scenery on her side, I saw that she wore the frown that preceded a large generalization.

"The rich aren't like us," she said at last.

"They aren't?" She shook her head. I got a firm grip on my kneebones and said, "Why not?"

"They pay less taxes." She murmured something about the injustice and perfidy of the world as she negotiated a series of potholes in the road. Then her tone softened as she continued almost wistfully, "We all of us have a hard time of it, rich and poor, in this vale of tears, so you can't blame anybody for squeezing all they can out of where you're going through only once. I can appreciate that even at my age. *Especially* at my age. So take what you can without hurting anybody else. Wear pearls and call the waiter over, if that's what you want. Live!" She bumped to a halt on the shoulder of the road again. "This is my last stop, and then I'll drop you at your street. Only be a minute."

I found myself before a liquor store on the city limits called The Spirit Shop. She dug the last carton of Bloody Mary Mix out of the back of the station wagon and bustled inside with it. She was beaming when she climbed in behind the wheel again. "Wanted to double the order this week. Sorry I couldn't oblige him, but I'll be back Monday."

Then her mood darkened mercurially again as we got under way, and I could sense she was debating with herself whether to communicate a last piece of information to me.

"I don't know as I ought to tell you this," she said at last, "but I smell a rat with Ma Godolphin. You should know this if you're going to take the case."

"Is Heck mixed up with her?"

"You've got that on your plate. He's an attractive man, of course, no more into middle life than Ma, who's also good-looking, as you'll find. But that don't explain his getting into her circle as fast as he did. Not just the smart set as such, but the in-group, they call them, inside even of that. Part of her — what do they call that again? The bunch that traipses around town behind artists and celebrities and stuff?"

"Entourage?"

"That's it. Well, Heck's made entourage, with Ma, but why? I think it's to soften him up for the takeover. You'll just have to sniff that out for yourself."

"You mean she's got her eye on the farm?"

"A cigar for the gentleman. Go to the head of the class. That's her game I'll bet my bottom dollar. And you better believe it and you better bear it closely in mind in arbitrating this case."

"I think there's some mis —"

"It may be a key factor. Well, forewarned is forearmed, and here's your place. Nice meeting you, and we'll be seeing you again soon. Bye, Doctor Bumpers."

On the sidewalk, I hesitated.

"By the way, Mrs. Sigafoos, are you from around these parts? I mean originally?"

"Well, yes, in general. I'm a native Iowan, but I wasn't born here, exactly. And it wasn't yesterday."

I had to ask the question. Clutching the door handle, I said, "Where were you born, exactly?"

"Dubuque. Well, I'll be suing you."

I ran up the stairs two at a time to the safety and seclusion of my office, where I sat for a long while trying as calmly and intelligently as possible to sort into some kind of coherent perspective the events I had experienced and the problems into which I had been precipitated.

3

WHAT MAKES A MAN CHOOSE A PROFESSION? WHAT IMPELS him to select this one as against another at which he might be equally skilled (or inept)? Doctors are said to be basically motivated by the fear of death, psychiatrists driven into that branch of healing by some haunting cleft in their own psyche — a rather ironic form of sublimation when you come to think of it. Marriage counselors (ambulance drivers in the sex war is good!) are probably expressing a profound desire to help others that is yet intimately linked with that equally profound, but not so commendable, curiosity from which gossip is manufactured. The seamy side of the human garment that is nevertheless an integral part of that garment. Flying to help a burnt-out friend is part and parcel of the undeniable thrill attendant on hearing the fire engines go shrieking past our own house on the way to his. A more important question to be asked in the long run, of course, is whether or not you are any damn good at what you've picked. For the old woman's jovial parting shot had set me suddenly to wondering: *could* you be sued for malpractice in this line of work?

These and related thoughts were coursing through my mind as I paced my office a few days later, half hoping, half fearing, that the wife or the mother-in-law or both would call again. I paused at the window and gazed down into the street below. How many of those people hurrying by in the noonday bustle did I imagine I might really help? My interest in marriage, and the contemporary question of whether it can, or should, survive, is autobiographical enough, my parents having split up in my adolescence. The divorce was by no means as hard on me as had been the strains of membership in a family that should have been dismantled sooner; so that when I call myself the victim of an intact home — or even the beneficiary of a broken one — I'm not just perversely capsizing a cliché generally regarded as otherwise defining a filial end-product not in perfect working order.

There is, as you know, a glum school of thought that holds we are all alike casualties of the domestic lot, like the scarred protagonists of Eugene O'Neill's own autobiographical love-hate dramas. Yet name any alternative and what have you got but another mixed blessing (or qualified curse)? And the author of *Long Day's Journey into Night* also gave us *Ah, Wilderness!* Which O'Neill are we then to believe, the one echoing back to us the lacerating entanglements of close kinship, or the dramaturgical masseur gently stroking our nerve-ends with a cozy little taradiddle of a parlor comedy? Either? Or neither? Or both? Unhappy as I was under the parental roof, I found no haven elsewhere either. I was just as wretched at the prep school I couldn't wait to get back to, the headmaster of which was forever sending letters to my parents saying my grades were nothing to write home about. Though I sensed in my bones that my father and mother were better separated, the threat of dissolution came as something of a jolt. Like the sight of Mrs. Brown and her mother *both* climbing out of the station wagon across the street. I jumped back from the window in a reflex that will have to be its own justification.

After locking my office door, I slipped back into my swivel chair hoping to God they hadn't caught a glimpse of me at the window. Had the wife glanced up just in time to see me so ingloriously retreat? And did they think they could always simply drop in? Several minutes passed with no sound of their footsteps in the hall. I breathed more easily, and found myself able to muse, however ruefully, on what my dash from the window so vividly recalled, through a flash of mental association linking two moments of my life. To the first of which might be traced my birth as a marriage counselor, or at least the genesis of my ambition to be one.

I had been cultivating imperturbability in Muscatine, my own home town, this being the summer I turned sixteen, when I overheard my mother say to my father, "I want a divorce." I shot on tiptoe to the door of the parlor where this bombshell had been dropped, in time to see my father set his cup of cocoa on the table beside the chair in which he was rereading *Humphrey Clinker* and, with the deliberation on which I was perhaps unconsciously modelling my own, finish the sentence, and probably even the paragraph in which the news had caught him immersed, because he turned a page in order to do so before looking up and inquiring mildly, "Oh? On what grounds?"

"That you're fifty-three years old and have never yelled 'Bravo!' "

"Have you?" I said, smiling in the direction of my mother as I sauntered in with my hands in my pockets. She repaid the query with the typically humoring patience reserved for men who argued like women. "I was only trying to help. Maybe you can patch things up. I might suggest that one way to make a man yell 'Bravo!' is to get him to invest in the play."

I now suddenly saw that the objections my mother had for some years been putting forward to my father possessed a unifying thread, or motif. "He's never thrown a snowball at me," "He eats a club sandwich with a knife and fork — *a knife and fork!*" "Must you keep a necktie on until you go to bed?" and so on. At times she would hurl some literary authority into her cause. "As Cummings reminds us, who pays any attention to the syntax of things will never wholly kiss you." So that was it. She had never been wholly kissed, then, never tousled in a winter wonderland, been given a partridge in a pear tree. Was married to a man not certain whether he dared to eat a peach. Now he did promise to give her a divorce for Christmas — a whimsicality come too late. That was not the impromptu gaiety, the small dishevelling madness with which she had hoped he might one day vary the even tenor of his ways. "Haven't you ever wanted to order something not on the menu?" she once beautifully cried, flinging her arms abroad with a long silk scarf streaming from one hand — woman wailing for her demon lover, sort of. "Why don't you buy me a swarm of bees for my birthday!" Some of her accusations, of which the above is a fair anthology, were to be taken literally, while others, of course, were purely symbolic; but all were now seen as given definitive embodiment in the charge that he had never shouted "Bravo!" Hardly a legally recognized ground for divorce (though one would like to see a presiding judge have it dropped on his plate), it did have a kind of elliptical ferocity summing up not just him but herself too, and their union along with it — like a flash of lightning that lays bare an entire landscape in a way you had not seen before. What you glimpse in the instant has a sulphurous truth.

My fixing the time of the aspersion as having been hurled shortly after their return from a weekend in New York seeing all the hit shows may be one of those tricks of memory, logically selective but otherwise of no general validity. The thing is that my father was certainly not your Dionysian type, reading Smollett in a pinstripe suit complete with vest, his hair parted in the middle and his socks neatly arranged in a bureau drawer in rows according to their length — ankle, mid-calf, and knee. The most nearly rakish thing about him was the checked cap in which on alternate Sundays he bicycled off to play Parcheesi with Mrs. Winterhalter. Not much of a combatant in the sex war either, rather a draft dodger; at best — to hammer the metaphor into the next county — one with papers stamped Limited Service; content with an adroitly timed bit of ironically passive resistance, now and again; on the whole a rather starchless auditor of Mom's own well-constructed recitatives. I think she'd have preferred his scoring a point off of her oftener than was the case. Sometimes an episode would collapse in a healing absurdity. Once he was despatched to put her foot down to a next-door neighbor with whom we were feuding about a building variance in a boundary dispute having to do with his wanting to push his living room out to a point too close to the property line, or something. "Tell him to go to hell," she instructed. He did as bade. "And?" "He refused."

My most vivid memory of my father involves a scene prior to my own birth, so I should say my most vivid *picture* of him, as left us in a reminiscence of his own. As a World War II G.I., he was one of those fortunate few privileged to sit on the floor at 27 rue de Fleurus and hear Gertrude Stein say, "All modern art is based on what Cézanne failed to do." He didn't know what it meant. My mother professed to, but never got around to telling us. He didn't care what it meant, but I think he somehow sensed that life from that moment on was going to be all downhill.

"I've had it," my mother would say as she stared incredulously at the rows of socks, each pair rolled neatly into a ball with the tops turned down, and the rows themselves further subclassified according to colors yet. She would gorge herself on the outrage a moment or two, before sliding the door shut with an unbelieving shake of her head. "Tick tock go my days, my years," lamented the romantic. "Tick tock, tick tock. I hear the metronome" — here flinging the braceleted arms abroad again — "but O God, where's the music!"

I hope that she has found that. She eventually married a businessman who swept her off to a branch office in Brussels. My father is living with the former Mrs. Winterhalter, in Muscatine still. I have drawn my own clinician's moral from the fated marriage. It's important for each of us to have both the Dionysian and Apollonian elements present in his makeup. But the mixture won't work between two people one of whom supplies the one while the other is all the other.

⊙⊙⊙

Footsteps could be heard mounting the wooden stairway to my floor, breaking off my revery. They were clearly made by two people, fortunately breaking step on that rickety ascent. I shot out from behind my desk on tiptoe to make sure the door was locked, then flattened myself against the wall beside it so as to cast no shadow on the frosted pane. The double tread beyond it drew nearer along the passage. Stopped. I held my breath, quiet as a mouse. The knob was turned. Then there was a knock on the door. The knob was rattled again.

"We know you're in there, Doctor Bumpers."

I unlocked the door and flung it wide.

"Oh, it's you two. I was just . . . And things have been so . . . Come in, come in!"

As we seated ourselves I took hasty note of their clothes. Mrs. Sigafoos sported her Land's Sakes trademark, but other than the poke bonnet and half specs there was nothing unusual about the way either was dressed. Under the light tweed coats lurked no T-shirts or sweatshirts, just flowered cotton prints. I looked across my desk from one to the other, raising my eyebrows inquiringly as I matched up my fingertips.

"Well, he's pitched us another curve," Hattie Brown began.

45

"Can you amplify? Be a little more explicit?"

They plunged into the latest instalment of the Heck Brown saga almost as a team, the wife relating developments for which the mother provided analytical insights.

It seemed that at dinner the other evening at Mother Sigafoos's, to which the farmer had "brung" a Châteauneuf-du-Pape to go with the pot roast that had been foretold, he had told them out of a clear sky — or as clear as could be expected in face of the Evergreen paperback in which he'd remained immersed at meat — that he had a block about farming, and thought he would like to lie fallow for a while. They had his number right off, the mother interpolated, oh, didn't they just! Was he using the term as a tiller of the soil applying to himself a metaphor derived from his fields? Not a bit of it. It was just another of the expressions he had picked up from the crowd he was running around with in town, among whom there was no end of artists and writers. They were forever having blocks and lying fallow. They were famous for it, as Mrs. Sigafoos knew from snatches of conversation caught while passing appetizers on terraces like Ma Peckinpaugh's, or at office Christmas parties at Old Mother Hubbard's dog food cannery. Whether such spells of inanition were justified by the bursts of creativity with which they alternated was a moot question, and not our problem here. Our problem here was what to do about the farmer, to say nothing of the farm! What must be our next countermove?

I rose and paced the office for a bit, pausing by the window once to twitch a blind so as to let in a little more light.

"There are two alternatives open to us. Two options.

One, you, Mrs. Brown, make an effort to fit in with the new crowd he's running around with, to adapt yourself to his new life-style — the worldliness on which he preens himself. This rover comes over. Or two, go on persisting as you have in your attempts to coax *him* back to the way you've always lived up to now. But let me ask you something. I'm curious about the emphasis you place on this fast crowd as having their coffee later, instead of with the meal. I see now that it does divide society in two. But do you have any theories about exactly why it is an earmark of sophistication, much less the beginning of the end?"

Here again she let her mother carry the expository ball, though occasionally interjecting a remark of her own. Mrs. Sigafoos had after all in her capacity as domestic *served* coffee later, and had observed close up the ilk who drank it then, and their instructive contrast with folk who still had it with the meal, of whom she remained steadfastly one.

Coffee later led to, if it was not already symptomatically part and parcel of, a certain loitering, lollygagging loosened moral fibre. It was only a question of time till brandies and cordials were sipped with any demitasses dawdled over later, and dispensing all of these, against her will, Mrs. Sigafoos had often got an earful of what went on in such a Babylonian atmosphere. Stories were told within women's hearing, then by women themselves. Modesty was going, going, gone, and could chastity be far behind? Many's the canoodle she had seen get started in that climate, as the brittle dialogue snapped and crackled like a brush fire. "I hear he's in Valerie's Out Basket . . ." "Has the divorce been solemnized yet? . . ." "He's keen on urban affairs — not that he doesn't have a thing or two going in the country as well . . ." "Their marriage is of course made possible by a grant from her father . . ." "If she wants to remarry now's the time to do it, when she has maximum trade-in value. But we must allow for her, shall we say, all-embracing spirit." The late lollygagging led to late arising, and that to not coping. Nobody coped any more. If such people went to church it would be to one of those built on horizontal lines by a modern architect, no lines going upward to suggest aspiration, let alone the Gothic pointed arch modelled on hands folded in prayer.

Coffee-later people were also the "look" people, a word as cleanly dividing them from those who still said "listen" as the coffee later did from those still drinking it with the meal. The two classes were identical. "Look, can you come for dinner on the twentieth?" That type were also always saying — oh, she had observed them! — "tell me." "Tell me, how did you find Nassau?" And "forgive me," that was another. "Forgive me, but I couldn't help admiring your hair. Tell me, who does it?" Yes, they were all collectively the coffee-later, look, tell-me, forgive-me bunch — that was the social anthropology of it. But if they really wanted forgiveness, as well they might, how about sinking to their knees in a church having some vertical lines for a change, and asking for it from the Party who alone could give it? Instead they preferred to slip deeper and deeper into a way of life that led inevitably on from one self-indulgent fribble to another. It led to — whatnot! It led to mint-flavored toothpicks. It led to dog jackets — to dog colognes! One woman she'd worked for had a Chihuahua got up in both. It was no bigger than a rat — in fact Mrs. Sigafoos had once found it caught in a rat trap in the garage, rescuing it just in time.

She drew a long breath. I quickly put the question that had occurred to me early on in the avalanche of explication.

"You profess opposition to all that drinking, and yet you market your own Bloody Mary Mix."

"Oh, I don't oppose all drinking, any more than Saint Paul with his exhortation to take a little wine. Far from it! Have a relaxing cocktail, fine. My own doctor recommends it. I'm talking about the whole ball of wax. When farmers say look instead of listen, let alone tell you they haven't the vaguest idea, we're through. I mean it's Decline-and-Fall time, kiddies. The show's over. Music up and out. Fade to Nero fiddling on the roof. Cut."

I nodded thoughtfully, accepting her reply. My first basic question having been answered, and with such a wealth of illuminating detail illustrating such depth of sociological insight, I was ready to put my second. I again addressed it to Hattie Brown, in a manner leaving no doubt of my determination that this time she answer for herself.

"Tell me," I began, blunderingly enough, so that I hurried forward hoping that my *gaffe* would go unnoticed, though I saw Mrs. Sigafoos smile as she smoothed out the lap of her dress, "you seem to set great store by the idea of Heck's again reading the Bible the way it was meant to be read in line with your family traditions — as anything but literature."

"That is correct."

"Then let's take that option in the form of a bargain you

make with him. I mean I think we should be satisfied we've given your method all the try we can."

"What's the bargain?"

A look passed between me and the older woman, on whose face was a smile somehow communicating that she knew what I was going to say, and agreed in advance.

"Go along with it. Let him lie fallow for, oh, maybe six months, during which your hired man should be able to keep up with things. He's been doing most of it anyway, with your help. Heck's end of the deal is that he agrees to do what *you* want. Read the Bible straight through from beginning to end, just the way you used to, and not as literature or dipping or skipping, and no wisecracks about how Genesis drags in the middle and Deuteronomy is a bomb."

"Right!" the mother said with a brisk nod of concurrence. "Bring him back to square one. Anything can happen when it comes to religion. People have sudden experiences, revelations, visions — like that famous English writer on a visit to Palestine recently. It's worth a try. You never know. And you've got a, now, *quid pro quo* going for you."

The wife nodded thoughtfully. "And how can things get worse?"

"We'll see," I said.

☉☉☉

I was letting a smile be my umbrella on a rainy day when the telephone rang.

"Any more ideas, *Doctor* Bumpers?"

"Now what?"

It seemed the farmer had pitched us another curve.

Much to all of us's surprise, as the mother put it, he had agreed to the bargain. It was a deal. That was a month ago. He kept his end of it too, while Clem Clammidge the hired man and Mrs. Brown worked the farm. He read the Bible straight on from the beginning and skipping nothing, not even the begats, with a few of which he even tried to amuse everyone by intoning the names, keeping their spirits up in that way. It was when he was about a third of the way through the Old Testament that he threw the screwball.

He had from time to time been commenting, rather ominously it could be seen now in retrospect, on the prevalence of concubinage in the old Holy Land days, and it was when he was "up to his hamhocks" in the book of Judges, which contains some very lurid accounts of adventures with concubines, that he remarked that he might like to have one. It had been a viable system for the Jews. Why not again for us?

"There's a lot to be said for the custom," he said, pouring some Beaujolais at the luncheon table where he had spoken his mind. "These women weren't true wives in the sense of being legally married, and they did a lot of work around the place. What do you call it again, dear — pitching in? That was part of the deal. Part of that life-style."

"I'll have to talk it over with Doctor Bumpers," the wife said, and hotfooted it over to her mother's for a three-way telephone conversation with me. Mrs. Sigafoos had an extension in her bedroom. We must have an immediate council of war on this fresh crisis. That was the phone call I got in my office.

51

"So that's his little game," the older woman said. "A *ménage à trois* they call them."

"Where are you?" I asked from my end.

"At my house. Heck's over at Pretty Pass."

"What's that?"

"The farm, the farm. It's what he calls the place now. Got a shingle on the gatepost. Like you said, he prunes himself on being sophisticated."

"I didn't say that, exactly."

"Now, now, don't back out of it. Stick with what you said, which you were absolutely right. Have the courage of your convictions."

"All right."

"But he's a smart one, this buster. He's got more ideas than a cranberry merchant. We've got to act fast, but careful. We're walking on eggs, so help me, Hannah. How soon can you get out here, Doctor Bumpers? I've got something on the stove just now and can't leave."

I caught a glimpse of the shingle on the farmyard gate as I shot past it on the way to the mother's cottage, where the emergency conference was to be held. When I arrived the mother was explaining to the daughter the general principle of the *ménage à trois*, which she defined as "triangles that get along." She sketched in what she knew of the arrangement as among the latter-day trends and realities of which she caught increasing wind passing canopies in homes where known worldlings foregathered.

"Hold it," I interrupted. "You're going too fast for me. Let me get this straight. You mean you think he actually has a woman he wants to move into the house?"

"Of course he's got someone on the string. Let's get you

out of Muscatine and with it, shall we? You think he's just fascinated by the institution as such? Talking in the abstract? Phuh!" Standing in the center of the parlor, the mother turned from me to the daughter, who was seated on a large ornate horsehair sofa. "The quickest way out of this is straight through it. Make him lay his cards on the table. Find out who she is and then talk it over."

"You mean you think Hattie should go along with this?" I asked.

"What has she got to lose? I mean if there is this party he's got on the side, Hattie's better off with her in the house where she can keep an eye on her." Mrs. Sigafoos was wearing in this instance a white mobcap, which she stopped before a wall glass to give a corrective fidget. "But let it all hang out. Iron everything out beforehand, so everyone knows exactly where he stands and no funny stuff. She's a concubine, period. And God knows you can use some help around the place. This could be what saves the farm."

4

THAT WAS THE ASPECT OF IT ABOUT WHICH THERE APPEARED to be some doubt, however. Heck did have someone on the string, a sculptress named Opal Kitchener who happened to be entering a fallow period of her own, following the fatigues of a retrospective of her stuff where, in fact, the two had met. Whether the interlude of abeyance applied only to her work or might extend to household and barnyard chores as well was uncertain. Hattie was not optimistic but she was resigned, certainly after my explanation that, having clearly blown the first of our two options, we had no recourse but the second. "If you can't lick the smart set, you'll have to join 'em."

"All right, bring her around and let's have a look," she said to Heck. This in the course of a discussion at which it had been agreed I should be on hand as their marital adviser, and in order that I might maintain an intelligent grasp of the situation. Heck had pencilled me in for drinks, which he was now by way of shaking up, wearing a tan corduroy suit and a checked shirt open at the throat, around which a silk scarf was loosely knotted.

"She too will be 'having a look,' you know," he pointedly returned, setting the shaker down in time to pantomime the quotation marks with two fingers of each hand — a fad that had drifted West along with brittle conversation, according to Mrs. Sigafoos.

"Fair's fair, everyone's sizing everyone else up. I understand. When can we expect her?"

"I was thinking Fridayish. Let's make it again for drinks."

"All rightie."

"And let's try to get with it, beginning with no more 'all righties.' Sort of thing that grates on some people. We might also edit the house a bit. Get rid of those doilies and souvenir pillows. I mean we don't want poor Opal to think she's walked into a nineteenth-century horror museum, do we now?" Heck said with a wink at me. "The whole thing would crash on takeoff."

"What about the organ?" Hattie asked, pointing to an old harmonium in the corner.

"That can stay. It's camp, of course. Bumpers might take a whack at explaining all that to you. I've about given up."

"Will it be O.K. to play it?"

"Of course, of course, but *be amused*. Do it on two levels. That's what camp is really all about. I mean if you play like 'Where My Caravan Has Rested' or 'I'll Sing Thee Songs of Araby,' do it with your tongue as far in your cheek as you can possibly get it. Don't be like 'rendering a selection,'" he instructed, with more sign language to indicate the quotes. "Hell, maybe we can leave the doilies too. Anyway the ones on the chairs, they're so absurd. What does our friend over here think? What do you say, Bumpers? Are you pro- or anti-macassar?"

I shrugged, half miming a murmured reply that they were perhaps a borderline nicety of camp about which one shouldn't get too uptight. I had noticed that Heck himself didn't always keep his citified cool, sometimes backsliding as a result of the wife's strain on his urbanity. He probably liked her but hated having constantly to explain nuances that, thus requiring endless exposition, broadened rather than narrowed the gulf between them. To try to close that gap, or at least keep it from widening, would be one of my jobs.

"I think I get it," said the wife in any event. "Now is there anything else?"

"Yes. Keep your mother away. I mean she's got to be kept absolutely under wraps, and that's the bottom line. We'll book it for Friday at fivish. You come too, Bumpers, if you're free."

"I wish you wouldn't call me Bumpers," I said. "It gives me a sense of traffic jams, of those miserable family joyrides on Sunday afternoons best forgotten. Call me Bill."

"Righto." Heck turned to Hattie again and repeated, "Remember, no dropping in by your mother."

"Don't worry. My mother understands these things better than you think. She knows four's a crowd."

⊚⊚⊚

It was going to be touch-and-go, we all knew that. Nobody was deceiving either himself or anybody else. I felt a little sticky about showing up for the confrontation, but in the end decided I should be on hand at occasions like this if

I was going to help keep this marriage from coming un-glued. It was finally agreed that, instead of Ms. Kitchener's coming just for drinks, we make a dry run of it with the whole weekend, which would give all concerned more of a chance to try things on for size. So when she arrived I helped show her with her two suitcases directly into a spare room upstairs. She was a sturdily built brunette of about forty, bearing a resemblance to Hattie for which I had scarcely been prepared, with the physique as essential to the large-scale spot-welded constructions in which she worked as it was to the farm chores on which Hattie pitched in.

As soon as she had freshened up and joined us in the parlor, Hattie bustled off to the kitchen to attend to some cheese puffs she had popped into the oven. Heck was shaking up some martinis. Opal strolled to the window to gaze out across the fields.

"What are you putting in this year, Heck? Alfalfa?"

"No, my dear, soybeans. Alfalfa's terribly *démodé*. Read any Department of Agriculture advisory on what to plant. Besides the ever-loving corn, of course."

"I see your hired man out there. Is he harrowing?"

"Oh, I wouldn't go so far as to say that. A trifle unpre-possessing perhaps."

Ms. Kitchener turned back into the room. "The Lomaxes are giving up their farm. Frank says it's because of the help problem, but I think he wants to chuck it with Cicely. Soo, another plum for Ma Godolphin to gobble up."

"Cicely is rather a dose." Heck stepped over to a low table on which he had set out four chilled glasses. "She says 'hubby' and 'comfy' and 'Literary Guild.' I mean what do you do when somebody you thought you knew joins the Literary Guild?"

Ms. Kitchener shrugged. "What is there *to* do? Life goes on as best it can."

Hattie now bustled in with a tray of the hot cheese dreams, wearing an asbestos kitchen glove I thought at first was a first baseman's mitt. She passed the appetizers around as Heck distributed drinks. Hattie set the tray down on a trivet and dropped into a chair to join the conversation. She was going to make every effort to get better acquainted with the other woman.

"What do you think of the new sexual freedom?" she asked.

"I think there's a lot to be said for it," the other woman replied. "The Puritan ethic has got to go."

"And the work ethic along with it," Heck said. "Let's not forget that while we're cleaning out the old attic. Well, mud."

"Mud."

"Likewise I'm sure," Hattie said.

We drank, from dry martinis mixed with pharmaceutical exactitude, and then a silence fell as we all set our glasses down. Hattie licked her lips. "My husband tells me your head is screwed on straight."

"And both feet are planted on the ground," Opal answered with a laugh.

"I hear tell your ancestors settled this part of the country. Mine did too, that's a coincidence. Well, we always tell a story about my great great grandfather. He came here from Virginia, raised sixteen kids, and said, 'That settles it.'"

"Oh, I *love* that. Heck, why haven't you told me what a raconteur you've got here? Anyway, Daddy quit the land, finally, after years of trying to develop a new hybrid strain of sweet corn. He said he was sick of pimping for yellow bantam."

"Oh, *I* see."

The conversation moved along through the usual unpredictable variety of subjects: a new artist in town who got his effects with an electric scalp vibrator; an acquaintance who had been kicked upstairs to a vice-presidency in charge of frozen hot *hors d'oeuvres* at Ma Godolphin's; a new movie in which civilization is taken over by pumpkin vines which, owing to an unexplained mutation, cannot be stopped.

After a fine dinner of roast lamb, for which Heck had selected a vintage Clos de Vougeot, we had our coffee and brandy in the parlor, where now in fact Hattie did favor us with a few songs on the old organ, which Ms. Kitchener had admired and coveted shamelessly. She played "Just a Baby's Prayer at Twilight," "Tell Mother I'll Be There," "Bird Songs at Eventide," "My Little Gray Home in the West," and "By the Waters of Minnetonka," making a great point of being terribly amused by it all as she pumped away at the pedals with her head thrown back, crossing her hands with mock virtuosity and maintaining an enormous bulge in one cheek by keeping her tongue thrust as deeply into it as she could throughout the entire rendition, according to instructions.

"I didn't mean *literally,* for God's sake," the poor farmer exclaimed the instant they were alone together in their downstairs bedroom, the other woman and I having retired

59

to ours overhead. Lying on the floor with an ear to a hot air register is a regrettable position for a marriage counselor to be in, but there it was. We were losing ground again. I perceived one of those terrible drains on his urbanity that kept setting us back no end. " 'Tongue in cheek' is just an *expression* we use, a term for — Oh, hell, what's the use," and he seemed to hurl some article of clothing, perhaps his trousers, against a wall. "This thing will never jell. I wouldn't give a dime for it." We had been thrown for a real loss.

"I suppose we'll just have to see," Hattie said. "I think I can get the hang of it, but it'll take time." I guessed she seemed more interested in the sounds of the other woman moving around in the guest room upstairs — next to mine as a matter of fact. I imagined the farmer's wife standing in her nightgown on a hooked rug. "What happens next? You going in unto her?"

"Oh, good God, I don't know," the poor farmer said. "There's probably too much static now. You play these things by ear anyway. You don't have a scenario, or get uptight about them."

"She won't come barging in here, will she?"

I could only imagine my client rolling his eyes to heaven with the "Deliver me" expression picked up from his fast friends in the city, as he plopped back into bed, pulling the covers over his head.

◎◎◎

Things were actually going a lot better than Heck imagined to be the case, as I was to sense in the weeks ahead when I was privileged to be a frequent caller at Pretty Pass. The gaucheries that galled him went almost unnoticed by the concubine, who often went around in a kind of abstraction anyway, perhaps mentally immersed in the configurations to which she would return once she was through lying fallow. She didn't offer to pitch in with the farm chores consequently left to the hired man, Clem Clammidge, and Hattie, but she more than pulled her weight around the house as a cook, rotating several specialties such as spaghetti Caruso, for which she always grated her own parmesan. Evenings after dinner, they all did pretty much what they wanted. Heck had discovered the pleasures of water color, at which he became fairly adept for an amateur thanks to help freely dispensed by Opal, who was in turn given valuable pointers by Hattie on the crewel work *she* enthusiastically took up. Perhaps the most charming manifestation of our *ménage à trois* lay in the sight of the three of them strolling along together in the evening air. At first the good folk about the countryside had been shocked. "It's called rural electrification," Heck had laughed as they promenaded by. But soon people looked out from their front porches and remarked nothing more than, "There goes that there *ménage à trois*." Of pioneer stock, they swiftly came to adopt a live-and-let-live attitude toward what was, after all, an attempt to push back the frontiers of human relationships.

It would be nice to take leave of our three there, strolling along in the mellow sunset light, like a fadeout in an old movie. Alas, an adder lurked in that paradise.

⊙⊙⊙

It was only increasing reliance on the hired man that kept the farm at all productive while the rest pursued their *dolce vita*. That had generated a feeling for him on the part of Hattie Brown, which was naturally deepened by working alongside him, as she often had to in order to keep up her end of the original bargain. She had therefore taken exception to the "harrowing" jest, as well as many another at Clem's expense. As a friend come often to Pretty Pass, I could sense this. As marital adviser I was steeled for the consequences: Mrs. Hattie Brown sitting across from my desk and announcing, "I think I'm falling in love with the hired man."

I rose and paced the office.

"This thing is snowballing," I said.

"The thing is what to do."

Mrs. Sigafoos was inevitably on hand again, and didn't she and I once more exchange glances indicating without a word that each was reading the other's mind, talk about rapport. It was she who spoke, though, proposing stratagems I daren't.

"Why don't you invite him in to dinner, and then to set a spell?"

"I doubt whether he'd fit in."

"He fits in with you. You cotton to him, anyone can see that."

The situation formulated itself instantly in my mind as an equation in human sensibility: Hattie was to the husband as the hired man was to her sophistication-wise. These relative levels of subtlety might be retained into infinity as each benefited from exposure to a higher — or the whole

thing might collapse in a heap. We must be extremely careful. We were taking a steep curve at high speed. We were
riding a tiger. We were a line of boxcars bumping each
other into the backside of beyond. Out of sight! The mother
spoke again.

"I've always hated to think of him batching it alone in
that one dinky room over the country store there, a mile's
walk to and from the farm where you give him one meal a
day — a lunch that he usually eats in the kitchen."

Seeing what was coming, I turned away with a quick
rejecting shake of my head, executing as I did so a dispers-
ing gesture. I was again washing my hands of this case. But
Mother Sigafoos plowed implacably on.

"You do have all those spare rooms going to waste."

"You mean as a *boarder?*" Hattie said.

The mother shrugged. "The more the merrier."

That put the cat among the pigeons all right! Clem was
an overflowingly friendly sort, with a broad smile and
bright white teeth giving the impression of numbering
more than the customary thirty-two. He was tickled to
death to be part of the group. You never knew what he was
going to say next, or do; given to no end of riddles and
japes and didoes. "Why will Ireland remain the richest
country in the world? Because its capital is always Dublin."
He had a racetrack routine about a mudder and its fodder
delivered in a crackling "Who's on first" crossfire that had
Hattie picking herself up off the floor in hysterics, but
through which the others sat with frozen faces over their
demitasses (contrived by Hattie by serving regular cups
half full).

63

"Now then," Clem said, approaching Opal with a pack of cards as he shuffled them. "Who'd like to play fifty-two-card pickup?"

"How do you play it?" she asked.

"Like this." And he deftly squirted the entire deck onto the floor at her feet, from between the thumb and fingers of one hand. "Now you pick them up."

"He's got to go," Heck said to his wife after a week of it. "And that's the bottom line."

"Then I do too," Hattie answered. "I like him. I think he's great gas. He grows on you."

It was a sticky situation. Four was indeed a crowd. Matters were only resolved when, a few days later, I heard that Opal Kitchener had announced she thought she would split for her city digs again. She had enjoyed her months here in the country, but she must be getting back to work. It was time.

"Well, your little ploy has paid off," Heck said to his wife when they were alone again at last. "Not that I'm all that sorry, frankly. Opal was getting a bit much at close grips, though I am fond of her. So O.K., your little trick has worked. Good old Clem has served his purpose as far as you're concerned. The old sock. But I suppose you'll let him stay the week?"

"More than that. I find him amusing. So we'll see what we see, play it by ear for a while, like you say. I know it isn't exactly what you had in mind, but it *is* a *ménage à trois*."

5

NOT THAT THE HIRED MAN HADN'T IN TURN HIS OWN LIFE OUT-
side the old farmhouse. That was how we were thriving in
the new weather. Having drawn surprised glances by a
passing allusion to penis envy he said, "I been seeing a
liberrian. You might as well know." This was shot rather
defensively from the bathroom, through the open door of
which the other two could see him shaving, in preparation
for an evening's dalliance elsewhere.

"It's not that, exactly," Heck somewhat acidly returned
as he rocked his after-dinner brandy in its snifter. "The
question we were rather revolving, don't you know, is
whether you mightn't have been born in a barn."

"Yeah," the other grinned back through a lathered face
as he nudged the door shut with one foot. "It's what must
of gave me my stable personality."

"He's got to go," Heck repeated to Hattie. "I've about
had it with that oaf."

"What'll we do without him?"

"What are we doing with him? He hasn't, speaking of
barns, cleaned this one out in weeks."

She nodded agreement, nursing a mug of cocoa. "He's anal retentive."

"Well, the horse isn't. You might mention some of these things while I'm away," Heck returned, not without marking her progress in getting the hang of intellectual conversation.

"When do you go to Majorca?"

"Friday week. Only gone two. I hope we can find somebody by then. The help problem is getting a bit much."

Briefed on these and similar scenes by Hattie, I was now squarely asked, in a spirit of flat professional confrontation, what we were to "do" about Clem Clammidge now that he had got too big for his britches.

Anyone with Psychology 3 on his credit transcript could see he was overcompensating for a keen sense of inferiority as — what? Why, the shlep of the group. That was surely why he was pounding his keyboard in the pursuit of obbligato affairs that he might, for the same reason, be exaggerating. Such was the obvious diagnosis. What was the cure? The troika might be saved if the hired man could be made less abrasive to the husband, who, to his credit, was as nettled on his wife's behalf as she was over Clem's cavalier treatment of her.

"Do your own thing" is a catchphrase by which we have been battered into intolerance. Yet is it such a far cry from Robert Frost's "Get something up for yourself"? Mother Sigafoos had got something up for herself, and there is nothing inherently wrong with a man turning boulevardier in middle life. Even the wife was clearly drawing some personal enlargement from those broadened horizons initially feared and deplored. That left the klutz, smarting under the knowledge of being that. What might he possibly get up for himself, or I help him get up, that would bolster his ego with some sense of self-fulfillment? A hobby, anything to confer a bit of the shine others around him were enjoying. I was about to pack it in, close the file on the Brown case convinced that we had reached a dead end and I could be of no further service, when I was seized with an inspiration.

The "thing" most people pursue will have something to do with the arts, for we must all be creative. So now there are more primitive painters than you can shake a stick at. We hardly need any more of them! No, what I had long thought we might use, as a counter-irritant, is a primitive critic or two. That was the bug I put in Clem's ear. With his sharp tongue and salty put-downs, he might be just what we need. A word to the wise was enough — at the first suggestion he was off and running.

The elements could not more auspiciously have combined for his debut. A new show just then coming up happened to be a retrospective by a local *naif*, a surveyor whose hobby had long been the easel. Black tie, so I got into a rented tuxedo in order to be on hand for the arrival of my protégé, who came, of course, in overalls and denim shirt. Hattie was on his arm, in a long blue dress. Clem was naturally challenged at the door.

"I'm from the *Wallaces Farmer*," he said. "We're covering these here events now."

"Oh."

The first picture he looked at, after accepting a catalogue, was a fish still life entitled "Salmon in Gouache." Clem contemplated it a moment, stroking his chin and then tapping his teeth with the brochure, and said, "Gimme sardines in oil." From a pillar behind which I could half conceal myself while watching his progress from entry to entry, I saw him move along to a painting of a horse, mostly a head protruding over a paddock fence. "A self-portrait I take it?" he said, and moseyed along to something else, wetting a finger as he paged through the catalogue.

By now he had excited considerable curiosity, which I stoked by slipping among the first nighters and asking in eager whispers, "Who *is* he?" As a result he soon collected quite a crowd, trudging in his wake and asking the same question among themselves and straining to catch his comments, wry or favorable. "I understand he's the critic from *Wallaces Farmer* or something," I told a tall bony woman in a pants suit. "Kind of thing we've needed for a long time, wouldn't you say?" "I certainly would," she answered with a nod, "after all the highfalutin jargon about art they've been feeding us. Excuse me, I want to get up closer to him."

Clem made his rounds of the gallery with a pack at his heels that by now included nearly everybody in the place. My own attention was drawn particularly to a stocky, sandy-haired man whose black tie was of the old-fashioned shoestring variety, who took the scene in with special intentness as he squeezed in slowly from the edge of the circle. He watched as Clem, now chewing on a matchstick, made for a picture at the end of the room. It was an oil of an old church pulpit executed in painstakingly literal detail, almost photographic in its facsimile likeness, as the catalogue copy pointed out. It was called simply "Pulpit" and Clem simply took the matchstick out of his mouth and said, "Pew."

The sandy-haired man darted forward and, seizing Clem's arm, drew him almost forcibly aside.

"How much is the *Wallaces Farmer* paying you?"

"Not 'nuff."

"I'll meet it, and more. How's a hundred and fifty a week?"

"Figure kind of drug in the middle."

"Two hundred."

"Still fantasizin' some."

"*Bugle*'s no *New York Times* you know. All right. Two fifty. It's my top figure."

"Your top's my bottom, but done and done. Plus expenses of course."

Thus was born the country's first primitive critic as Clem went to work as columnist for the *Daily Bugle*. The culture editor, whose name was Ed Slocum, didn't in the least mind he'd been had about the *Wallaces Farmer* fib, indeed he welcomed a truth which removed the single tarnish on his journalistic "first."

Cousin Clem, as he signed his stuff, became a familiar figure and enjoyed a considerable vogue as he gallivanted about the town and even the countryside, dressed for gallery premieres in the overalls in which he'd made his debut, to which a bandanna knotted at the throat was added, or, in the winter months, the plaid mackinaw and matching cap with earflaps that became his alternate trademark. One show he presently covered exhibited the recent pieces of a surrealist celebrated for his "eerie nuances," as the catalogue copy put it. "Them nuances look like the same old ances we been getting from Dali and Tanguy," Clem drawled, pitching an apple core into a sandpot as he moseyed on out the door.

There were surprises from this "Grandma Moses of exegesis," as he was called. One sculpture show certainly expected to draw his fire did nothing of the kind. The gallery in question was entirely taken up with pedestals on which no figures whatsoever reposed, from one to another of which art lovers strolled reading catalogue copy which ran: "In his mature period, Kublensky has aimed at a progressively more drastic refinement of the principle of minimal form. Thus an area of virgin space unoccupied by anything save what the viewer himself might imagine it to contain, rather than what the artist has arbitrarily imposed, came to represent to him the ultimate distillation of linear values." Titles conducive to private improvisation were supplied on small brass plates affixed to the pedestal tops. "Gloucester Fishermen," "Ped Xing," "Mrs. Rumpelmeyer's Flesh," and "Feigned Orgasm" were a few over which people especially loitered, the last two being among those quickly acquiring the red stars indicating purchase. They stood immersed in "visual rumination" for periods longer than would be provoked by bromidic representation, as images materialized on the inner eye — the means by which the artist had at last managed to "make the viewer a collaborator in the creative process." Other favorites were "The Old Tehachape Glee Club," "The Things You Make Me Do, Mrs. Remoulade!" and "Shortstop with Glockenspiel." Also popular, and eventually snapped up, was a surrealist piece whose phantasmal juxtapositions were suggested by the title, "The Jockey Is Haunted by Dreams of Getting into the Horsey Set."

Cousin Clem was by and large affirmative.

"Had to be expected. Inevitable. After all the years artists have been telling the subject matter to get lost," he wrote in the *Bugle*, "this was like a tin can tied to a dog's tail — bound to a cur (bound to occur). Me, I kinda took a special shine to 'Feigned Orgasm' (though I fancy some folks didn't think it quite come off), '*Hommage à Fromage*' (with its echoes of what Churchill said on being told the French made two hundred and eighty-five different kinds of cheese — 'Any nation that makes two hundred and eighty-five different kinds of cheese is ungovernable'), 'Whose Eyelashes Are These?' 'Why, You — !' and 'Good Old Bosom Bread.' I thought 'Voltaire' less successful on the whole, while 'The Butter Churn' struck me as a rather contrived exercise in the nostalgia of which we've all had rather a snootful, 'ppears to me."

He also dug an art happening scheduled to take place at high noon of the next Saturday in front of the City Hall, where the artist in question had promised to paint his car with oleomargarine, according to handbill announcements that had been widely distributed. I was on hand as my protégé's most ardent fan, taking a position near the pillar against which he negligently leaned, chewing a toothpick. The artist, a man named Cory Gluckstern, did drive up as scheduled, parking his Chevrolet sedan at the curb. He sprang out with a large bucket and brush, slathered the automobile from bumper to bumper, passed the hat, bowed

71

to the onlookers, and drove off to a round of applause. A woman in a flowered straw hat was very angry.

"Why paint an automobile with margarine?"

"It's cheaper'n butter," Clem said.

The rest became swiftly history. The Horace Pippin of criticism, as he was sometimes alternatively called, reached perhaps the peak of his first vogue with an article entitled "Why Sculpture Ain't Statuesque no More," which was widely reprinted in even more than the dozen or so dailies to which his column was by now being syndicated. Many dined out on it, not least of course the hired man himself. Hostesses fought to snare him for dinner parties, the farmer's wife and the librarian he also continued to fancy vying for his favor as he squired now one, then the other to whatever opening must be attended over increasing areas of the countryside. Occasionally still another woman would sit, helmeted and goggled, behind him in the Honda on which he tooled away to his cultural chores. His spare time was spent in reading the work of other critics and of art historians in general, whether in book or journal form, so that, once again, the farm labors were neglected. Hattie, often to be seen driving the tractor with her hair in curlers, was glad to see the winter come again, when the farm need not be worried about as much as otherwise.

One evening the hired man was slated to catch a retrospective with a snowstorm definitely threatening. It began in the gloaming, in keeping with memories resonant enough with menace, and the wife urged him to skip it till later. But he had come to set great store by his premiere appearances. "Sort of a Charles Burchfield storm," he observed, hunching into his mackinaw as he looked out the window at the thickening flakes. He wasn't going to escort anybody, which was fortunate for the ladies omitted, as he damn near got marooned in a blizzard that knocked the power out for square miles around. With the oil furnace off, the house was like a butcher's cooler when he finally made it back home, around two A.M., and he climbed gratefully into bed with the other two in the downstairs bedroom, the only one left remotely tolerable thanks to the nearby fireplace.

"Were you gonna send the Saint Bernard out after me?" he said as he got in beside the wife.

"How was the show?" she mumbled sleepily.

"Well, this gink clearly derives from Mondrian, the most neglected linoleum designer of our time, have I told you?" In shoving over to make room for him, the wife in turn pushed the farmer against the wall, exciting an impatient grumble from that quarter.

"You can have my share of Mondrian anyways," the hired man went on, warming his cold feet on hers. "Officially renouncing the curve, like he done in mid-career, vowing to draw henceforth nothing but straight lines and right angles, don't endear him to me none." He gave an especially pleasurable nuzzle. "Thank God *you* ain't all right angles," he chuckled, tweaking her some.

"For Christ's sake, it's two o'clock!" the farmer said. "Could we postpone this no doubt stimulating discussion till tomorrow do you think? I mean I don't want to be a party pooper or anything."

"We won't let it get around," said the hired man, who was also doing his best to get the hang of brittle dialogue. "Did you know that these here crazy quilts are now regarded by abstract expressionists as folk cubism? Lot to be said for that. Not sure as I can give it my blanket endorsement though."

"Judas Priest!" the farmer said, losing ground again as he reclaimed his share of the covers with a vehement jerk.

"Well, good night and keep cold, like Robert Frost said to the fruit trees for the winter, if memory serves," Clem chatted, showing the influence of the librarian again. "How does it go again? Dread fifty above more than fifty below."

The farmer flung the blankets back and heaved himself out of bed.

"I've always liked 'The Death of the Hired Man,'" he said quietly as he got into his bathrobe and slippers. "If the Thanatopsis Club is going to remain in session, I hope you'll excuse me while I go fix myself an Irish coffee. *If* I can find the Sterno."

"Keep in touch, won't you," Clem said.

◉◉◉

So it seemed my therapy had backfired again. Clem was more insufferable than ever. Instead of success mellowing him thanks to the liquidation of a sense of inferiority, he was arrogating to himself the time-honored prerogatives of talent. (When the tough get going, the going gets tough.) He might yet pull the plug on all of us. Rather than stilling the beast heard clanking its chains inside him, I seemed to have created a monster threatening to overrun the countryside. His snobbery was notorious, with a sort of *enfant terrible* unpredictability about it, so that hostesses who had feared his "regrets" were apprehensive of what he might say or do once he did show up. He might rise from a dinner table and think he'd shove along to another. "Firm believer in the two-party system, you know, so I reckon I'll toddle over to see what's cooking at Mrs. Cahoon's." Or he might ask another guest what she was doing after the orgy.

What still kept him relatively in line was his by no means showing any signs of penetrating the ultimate in-group, Ma Godolphin's retinue, known as the Elect (recalling Proust's "Faithful" coterie) among whom Heck Brown himself remained a regular. This enabled Heck to preserve the pecking order on which he was damn well determined. Yet by the same token there *was* such an order, in a *ménage* in which Clem kept an upper hand over Hattie by virtue (if that's the word) of his insistence on a free run with other women. And unabating competition from the widening celebrity on which Clem now naturally "pruned" *him*self guaranteed ever-intensifying psychic strain in the already complex pattern within whose subtle tissues we were all caught up — for I was no longer a bystander. Professional integrity demanded that I pitch in and go to work myself on the farm that had become a shambles. I could offer no less to the two women the day they once again toiled up the stairs to my office for a further review of a rapidly deteriorating situation, and fresh counsel. They declined my offer, insisting that we try first to find another bona fide hired man. The first order of business, in any case, was to relate a bitter quarrel between Clem and Hattie, in the course of which account I was able to see what tremendous strides Hattie had made in getting with it.

"He interiorizes," she tearfully protested.

"There, there," Mrs. Sigafoos said. "I know."

"While at the same time accusing *me* of interiorizing."

75

"Taking everything personally, like they use to say us women do. Doctor Bumpers may have something to tell us about that, all right. But what else? Let it all out."

"You're a sex object, and that's it. He gratifies himself on a surface level, but what about you." Hattie tweaked her nose with a handkerchief. "It's not right. A woman is like gazpacho. She should be stirred from the bottom."

"There, there. I know."

"To him women are like awnings. Meant to be let down."

"Beast."

"I'm not going to be the auxiliary ego."

"Or play second fiddle neither."

"Being in the public eye —"

"Like grapefruit — he's a squirt."

"— has only brought out his latent male chauvinism, which fits in with his whole macho mystique."

"Leaving you home at night to read."

"All this image. He's become a photo-mural of himself."

"And meanwhile what about the farm. I'm for the new emerging American woman too, and it gives me pleasure to see you out there on the tractor in a leather mackinaw, or strewing caution to the wind like feed to the chickens. But you can't do it alone."

"Maybe that's where I can help," I said. "It's the least I can do. I'm not so busy at the moment that I can't manage, say, two days a week — "

"No, first I have a better idea. It just came to me. Charlie Achorn. Why don't we ask him?"

"That shirtsleeve philosopher?" the daughter asked.

"Yes. What could be more down-to-earth than that. He's not working now, I see him hanging out around the stores talking on subjects. But he will work. I know people who've hired him. He won't stay, but he's good for a spell. 'I'll give you an honest day's work. 'Course I ain't sayin' how long it'll take me, but I'll give it to you.' But that's just his style, that foxy stuff. But he'll work. And anyhow, what can we lose?"

"We'll see," I said.

6

NOW, I HAPPENED TO KNOW ABOUT THE CRACKERBARREL PHI-
losophers, whom I had not neglected in my studies of the
city. None had moved with the times more than they, yet in
an era of rapid and widespread fragmentation they alone
seemed to retain their cohesion and identity as a peer
group. Never more than four or five in number, they would
sit on tilted chairs encircling the Today's Special bin at the
supermarket, or, whittling or not as the mood betook, dis-
pose themselves on the broad front stoop, from which with
perverse leisure they would lift their feet to accommodate
shoppers trundling carts in or out through the electronic
doors. Their relative stability made their relationship to the
surrounding community somewhat that of a Greek Chorus,
as they commented on what they observed or heard in
tones whose pungency could be taken for granted. It was
they who in rotation supplied the Dial-a-Saw feature in-
augurated as a telephone advertisement by the supermarket chain itself. "You may be a pistol without having an
aim in life," and so on. That sort of thing they did for

cakes — their own real aim in life being to perpetuate a timeless folk tradition; except that they brought it sharply up to date by airing the more abstruse and esoteric elements in contemporary thought and art (taken note of by others merely in the superficial form of sweatshirts, T-shirts and posters).

They were sprawled out in the early afternoon sunshine the day Hattie and I went to town on our mission, three-strong, coining maxims and trading philosophical observations in a taunting crossfire that marked them peppery as well as salty: disputants to be taken on only by each other, by anyone else at his peril. We stood nearby at a row of shopping carts, pretending to review our marketing lists while we got an earful, particularly of Charlie Achorn who happened to have the floor when we drew up.

"Caught with your Kierkegaard down that time?" he was drawling with a rather malicious grin. This to Ham Abernathy as the one best versed in the father of existentialism, as well as such followers as Jaspers, Heidegger and Husserl in Germany, and Sartre, Camus and Marcel in France. Abner Teasdale, a Socrates saddled with a Xanthippe who had by now made a quirt of his own tongue, had just bested him on some fine point of existential thought.

"All goes back to Vaihinger's 'As if' philosophy o' course, you old galoot," said Ham, who sat back against the brick wall in patched dungarees and a decayed straw hat through holes in which wisps of red hair protruded. "Intellectual postulates and even mathematical categories are plumb fictions, 'ccordin' to him. Ever read Sartre's *Being and Nothingness*, Abner?" The question was addressed with a show of amusement at his asking it at all. "Well, he goes plumb into the whole multi-level reality of existence, including role playing. Sartre makes the point that not even a waiter can *be* without playing at being. So I reckon we can let you play at being a philosopher, Abner."

There was a moment of silence such as often punctuated their forensics, in which the supposedly deflated Abner rallied his forces, at last drawling, " 'Ppears to me you yourself forget what Camus says in *The Myth of Sisyphus,*" adding with a reimbursement of the other's irony, "Sure you recall the passage I mean, Ham. Part where Camus defines man's pride as 'fidelity to his limits.' " That another zinger was due he telegraphed by typically turning his head to fire a jet of tobacco juice into an adjacent patch of grass. " 'Course it poses a problem if the man hisself is the limit."

Having got his own back, Abner pressed his advantage by switching the subject to T. S. Eliot as non-Kierke-gaardian, rather than anti-Kierkegaardian, Christian, a brief segue serving in turn as a springboard from which to launch his imitation of Eliot reading "The Waste Land." Ham cut into this apparently all too familiar shtick to say, "Poetry ain't my forte and Eliot ain't exactly my turf, but I do seem to recall the poem is a epic. You aim to afflict us with total recall, Abner?" Here Achorn butted in. "Oh, I reckon he'll cut it some as he goes along, same as Ezra Pound done. By the way, I ever tell you boys about the time I put one over on old T. S.?"

"No but you will, Oscar, you will. That's what Whistler cracked to Wilde, you know —"

"Well sir, Eliot was booked into the university here on a reading tour. I went. Read from *The Four Quartets.* Usual reception afterwards for him and the then new Mrs. Eliot in the faculty lounge, and there was the *rara avis*, namely Eliot, in the flesh, on a sofa everyone was leavin' to the two of them, out of awe? Someone had to break the ice, so I sat down there to try to make them feel at home. I never found the famous 'magisterial stare' all that magisterial. Anyways, I had my copy of the *Quartets*, which he seemed tickled to death to autograph. We chewed the rag some about the objective correlative and his debt to Laforgue and one thing and another, and then I says, 'Tom,' I says, 'if I may call you that, a body can't but be struck by the heap of marine imagery in your poetry. It's seven eighths water, like the earth itself.' He chuckled at that, as did the missus. 'Now in the "Dry Salvages" one, which you read beautifully I thought, you give a kind of special emphasis, or fondness, to the line "The river is within us, the sea is all about us." Here I began to tease him a mite. I says, 'Might the particular river within you be not just no abstract river but' — I give him a sly sidewise look — 'the Mississippi?' Then I looks at him even askancer, so askance I nearly lost sight of him, and says, 'Might what you've got eatin' you be a slight case of the St. Louis Blues?' He allowed that was mighty sharp of me."

"Oh, you're sharp all right," Ham said from under the straw hat. "You're so sharp every time a guy shakes your hand he has to bandage a couple fingers."

"And with that Eliot snatched the book back from me, turned to the passage in question, and scratched out 'starfish' and writ in 'catfish.' Fact. I'll show you two frauds the book if you don't believe me."

Ham rose and stretched, yawning cavernously.

"Banking on the phenomenological doctrine that objects have no existence apart from the observing consciousness, I take pleasure in making you two varmints vanish into thin air by shoving along to the Here and Now and wet my whistle."

"Reckon I'll join you," Abner said, climbing to his own feet. "Meant to ask Louie last time what the vintner buys that's half so precious as the stuff he sells. Clean slipped my mind. So long, Charlie."

That left Achorn, propped against the wall scratching on the back of an envelope what might be a new batch for Dial-a-Saw. Hattie threw an inquiring glance at me, who nodded agreement that now would be the moment to strike.

"Charlie Achorn!" she said as we stepped forward together.

He got to his feet with visible reluctance, pocketing his literary materials.

"Afternoon, ma'am."

"I'm Hattie Brown. Remember me? Living on that farm just past Finley Forks."

"I have a poor memory for names, though I can never recall a face. Still it rings a bell."

"And this is Doctor Bumpers, a friend of the family."

"How are things?"

"Actually we need some help out there. Badly. I know you do hire out now and again, so if you're not busy just now, we'll pay you the highest going rate, and I think you'll find the company stimulating."

He removed his hat and with the same hand rummaged a moment in his mop of thick brown hair. "Give you a day's work, provided you don't trouble too much about exactly how long it takes —"

"Yes, I know all about that. Could you maybe run out with me now, and see the place? I just want to lay in a few supplies."

"Reckon it's what you'll find me layin' in, often as not. 'Specially the bottled."

◉◉◉

That was just Achorn's style, as the mother said, the need of one whose terrible mission it is to strew the world with rejoinders. He could deliver the goods when he had a mind to, and so consequently things eased up once more on the labor front — alas, with further complications to the domestic.

Hattie hadn't realized how true it was that he would "find the company stimulating." He sensed instantly the updated Brook Farm experiment into which we had now more or less inadvertently slipped (or evolved, as you wish), and he gave instant notice of wanting to be part of the group. Not in so many words, but with suggestions and innuendoes about which there could be no mistake. His admittance was the price for his remaining aboard the tractor. There would be no getting out of it if the farm was to go on being profitably worked so all concerned could pursue their own brands of self-fulfillment. So he checked out of the residential hotel where he'd been batching it and joined what now had, as I say, all the earmarks of a commune.

To the colony's ideal of easy intellectual camaraderie and egalitarian sexuality he swiftly contributed his share. This was principally true at dinner, to which he was at first admitted over Heck's dead body, and where, seemingly oblivious of giving aggravation there, he would sit expounding Beckett or Unamuno, or threatening recollections of Eliot or Eric Hoffer or Evelyn Waugh. He was one of the few people Waugh could bear to have around in the last years when Waugh was holding the world at bay, to hear him tell it. The stories he told did have a ring of authenticity about them, certainly those I heard the night I again had the pleasure of dining at Pretty Pass.

"I mind the time Evelyn and me was sipping our port in his study one afternoon," he said, licking the foam from his lips after a copious swig from the stein of beer to which he was partial at meat, while the others watched transfixed. "He reached over to a table and tossed me a new novel the American publishers had sent him, in hopes of a blurb of course. He give 'em a blurb all right. He wrote back, 'This reads like creative writing.'"

Achorn chuckled at the memory, as did we all. Except for Heck who I noticed out of the tail of my eye was gripping the table edge in both hands, as though preparatory to overturning it. We were losing ground again. Already unhappy over the white Burgundy he had uncorked for the rest of us, he had murmured something about having a Beaune to pick with his vintner. It gave one again a glimpse of the throwaway grace notes that had enabled him to make entourage with Ma Godolphin; you could also see he was on the verge of blowing that hard-won cool again. We all felt thrown for a loss when that happened to our bellwether.

"By unspoken agreement we kept off the subjects of politics and religion. Still in all, him and Eliot were two who could fall into the arms of the church without falling into its hands, *n'est-ce pas?*" He recalled Eliot's tact the night of the reception in coping with a local poet notorious for mooching small sums on short notice. "He's a first-rate sponge," Achorn said, impaling a boiled potato on his fork, "but a second-rate Spender," he added, baring, in a prolonged in-joke grin, a jumbled assortment of putty-colored teeth.

"Judas . . . Purriest," Heck said as he slammed his napkin down and rose and went off to the adjacent parlor.

I remained in my chair, undecided as to what course of guidance to offer in this admittedly thorny stage in everyone's development. I think we all sensed Heck to be listening intently in the other room, his attention speared in spite of himself. Cousin Clem sent the conversational ball rolling in its next direction. He said that as to Eliot, whom he'd only lately taken to reading in the belief that arts other than his own should be kept in touch with in the interest of balanced judgement, he for his part preferred the satirical verses of the early period. "Like I got a special bang out of Mr. Apollinax, whose 'laughter tinkled among the teacups.'"

"Well, that's Bertrand Russell he's portraying there," said Charlie Achorn, who then launched a personal reminiscence of his own concerning Russell, who had been his vis-à-vis at a sit-down dinner for seventy given by a mutual friend in London. He remembered it as one of those happy occasions when two kindred spirits hit it off instantly.

"When he learned I was a philosopher too, we were off and running on some of the trickier problems of epistemology. What do we really know, like about the age-old distinction between mind and matter. 'What is matter?' Russell says, and I says, 'Never mind.' And he says, 'What is mind?' and I says, 'That's no matter.' Bertie, you called him that on short notice, thrun his head back in stitches — speaking of laughter tinkling among the teacups."

From the parlor came a loud flat *splat* of a sound, as of a newspaper or magazine hurled violently against a wall by someone being worn thin by the strains of life in a utopia. Hattie rose and hurried into the other room. I followed, motioning for the others to continue as though nothing were amiss.

Heck, who must have regretted his impulse even before the *Rolling Stone* struck its objective, was to be seen tidying it back into the magazine rack.

"What's the matter?" Hattie and I both asked.

"Matter, he's driving me bonkers. Both of them, if it comes to that. Absolutely *up* the wall."

"Why?" Hattie said. "I find him terribly amusing. He's a gas. If the new freedom —"

"*Why?* In the first place, if he's a shirtsleeve philosopher the least he could do is wear a shirt — at least at table. It should be *de rigueur* for the genre, wouldn't you say, while undershirts are definitely regarded as *de trop* in the best circles. Or am I being picayune? We'll leave it up to Bumpers here. What say, Bumpers, can you appreciate my finding it a little hairy here with these neanderthals around all the time?"

"The problems of compatibility, difficult enough in all conscience between two people, are bound to increase algebraically with every new party to a given combination," I said.

"And holding his cigar on a nail to smoke it down to the

nub. You might emphasize a few of these points in my absence. And those ridiculous 'reminiscences' of his. Do you suppose he imagines anyone seriously —?"

"When do you go to St. Tropez?" Hattie asked.

"Friday fortnight. If I can survive these two cornballs here."

"Well, there you are. You have your druthers, I have mine. I mean if we're going to talk about open marriage —"

Nothing could more have confirmed what was left implied than the phone call that interrupted her. It was Ma Godolphin, asking Heck to join her and a few others to catch a showing of *Animal Crackers* at a local movie house. That was the obligation that went with the privilege of inclusion in her entourage: an invitation was a command.

"Drop by for you in half an hour, Ma."

I took my leave soon after dinner, and it is from subsequent sessions with Hattie that I reconstruct the events in which that particular evening culminated for all those now at Pretty Pass.

⊙⊙⊙

It seemed Heck and the bunch in town caught the early show, stayed to see the first half again, then had a few drinks at the Here and Now. It was shortly before midnight when he returned, to find the rest all in bed together.

"And who is this, his steed foam-flecked?" Hattie called gaily over.

She was between Cousin Clem who, propped up on the outside edge and wearing a green eyeshade, was revising some copy with a pencil, and Charlie Achorn on her left, who had been discoursing on Martin Buber, with some personal sidelights on the Austrian philosopher, whom he'd met in Vienna. They were passing a half-gallon of red wine around, which Achorn offered to Heck, who for the moment declined with a shake of his head. His show of social status for the evening had made him considerably less defensive. He began to remove his coat and tie and set things on the chiffonier-top, preparatory to retiring himself, on lines they might very well see for themselves. A chicken roosting on a chair splat was trying to get some sleep in a corner of the bedroom.

"It's a modest little wine," Achorn observed, "and believe me no wine ever had more to be modest about."

"As one prime minister said about another, if I'm not mistaken," Heck murmured.

The jug had by now reached Cousin Clem, who paused in his jottings to deliver his own verdict.

"Cautious, even obsequious," he said after a sip or two. "Hedges its bets. Tries to weasel its way into your good graces. Don't really commit itself. Plays it safe till it sees. Pussyfoots. I don't like that in a zinfandel, or any wine for that matter."

Hattie put a question to Achorn. Who, of all the world figures he had known or met, struck him as the greatest thinker of our time?

"Without a doubt, Gandhi," he replied. "The single occasion I met him, we had a long and mutually profitable exchange of ideas. In the course of it, I ast him what he thought of Western civilization, and he said he thought it would be a good idea."

Heck smiled as he overturned his trousers and, clamping the cuffs under his chin, smoothed the legs down evenly, preparatory to letting them fall neatly over a hanger bar. There was certainly no doubt he was beginning to recover the aplomb that had been under such a terrible strain lately.

"Oh, really?" he said, his leisure illustrative of the silken guile of which he was capable in dealing with a sexual rival. "Then it's a remark he must have got off on innumerable occasions, as I've read it more than once myself." From inside the closet he added drily, "Not that it's not a mot worth repeating, of course."

He climbed over the others clear to his favorite wall corner, where, hooking on some reading glasses, he dipped into a little Auden. The bed as a consequence became quite crowded, but he adhered to an inflexible rule of occupying the preferred, so to speak senior, place whenever he wished, this being part and parcel of the pecking order he was determined no amount of group sex or erotic democracy was going to disturb, inconvenience to others be damned. It still left Clem on the hostess's right, the somehow more irritating Achorn on her left.

Aware that the name dropper had glanced over at what he was reading, he steeled himself for another reminiscence in raconteur form, but the danger passed. Inexplicably, he had never met the poet. Instead the wife spoke up.

"Things are getting a little kinky around here, wouldn't you say? Oh, do talk me out of this hoary viewpoint somebody. But where will it all end?"

Cousin Clem set the manuscript aside on its clipboard and doffed his eyeshade.

"Well," he said, "as the first voyeur said to the second voyeur, we'll adopt a wait-and-see attitude."

He gave everyone a lump of coal for Christmas, being just then especially enamored of fortuitous form.

7

BUT OUR CLEM WAS WHISTLING IN THE DARK, FOR ALL HIS progress in the new life-style and all the swath he was cutting there. I alone knew what was troubling him, in my steadily expanding role as collective confidant and lamp unto their feet.

His stuff was falling off. That was his boss Ed Slocum's term for a steady ascent into literary merit, for a detectable advance in subtlety, into an ever more sesquipedalian whatnot all of which Slocum lumped together as creeping sophistication. Good on the home front, bad news on the professional. That was it in a nutshell. As Slocum saw it, it was all part and parcel of what he deplored as a *knowledgeableness* of the contemporary scene drawn from the works of the standard critics in which our find had been mistakenly immersing himself. In short, he was becoming spoiled. That was the word Slocum laid bluntly on the line. He was no longer a primitive. Knowing Clem to be my creation, he confided all these misgivings to me, and then invited me to be present at a showdown session in his office where he intended to spell it all out in black and white for his staff critic.

"Like what the hell kind of talk is this?" Slocum read back some of Clem's previous day's column as Clem stood on the other side of his desk, in a tableau quite clearly indicating he was on the carpet. " 'Them visual verities and that there implicit trust in the hegemony of the random carry suspicious echoes of Max Ernst's early experiments with *frottage* they call it, rubbings taken off different objects and then developed with conscious technique from the original, duh, happenstance.' " Slocum, in a striped silk shirt with sleeve garters, looked up. " 'Implicit trust in the hegemony of the random,' Clem?" he said, his bloodhound eyes sad with reproach. " 'Successfully disinfected of subject matter'?"

"Why, what it means, Ed —"

"I don't give a damn what it *means!* That's not the point. The point is I pay you to talk United States, and Boone County United States at that. This gibble-gabble I can get a dime a dozen. You were a real find," he continued in a mixture of indignation and sorrow, snapping his galluses as he paced the office. "A breath of air, a genuine colloquial. A real First as it turned out, and a feather in my cap even more than in Doctor Bumpers's, maybe, being as how I laid out the money and really put my neck out. It ain't often you put your neck out and get a string of pearls. Now the pearls turn out to be — cultured! Now you wind up dishing me the same old twaddle we're trying to get away from."

"Rosenberg —"

"Oh, to hell with Rosenberg. And all the rest. That's just what I mean. If I wanted their jargon I'd hire them — and

I advise you to stop reading it, if that's what's got into the woodpile. And this." Slocum picked up another column from the sheaf of clippings on his desk. " 'Applying the paint to the nude model and then hurling her onto the canvas, like Plonka done in his middle period, got us some right dynamic blotches at least as arresting, believe you me Sister Sue, as the labored contrivances of the abstract expressionists, while triumphantly dichotomizing subject and object in a use of the fortuitous not unakin to the so-called aleotoric music of composers who utilize everything on the score sheet, flaws in the paper, flyspecks, you name it, as notes to be played by the instrumentalists.' " Slocum paused for breath and instantly resumed with a mounting sense of personal outrage. " 'Now this gink's perverse color juxtapositions, mangled perspectives and anatomical deformities serve to rout any lingering aesthetic pieties you or me or Aunt Frigadella might harbor, seems like. Taste must go. That is what them ornery forms and representational claptrap, such as the urinal motif, say. It ain't enough, Plonka 'ppears to be telling the nostalgist hung up on Truth and Beauty, to suspend disbelief. We gotta suspend belief itself.' "

"You'll notice I —"

Slocum gave one angry jump, like a kangaroo. "You don't preserve your purity by throwing in a few 'gottas' and 'ginks' and 'dad-blasteds' here and there," he exclaimed, overriding the anticipated defense. "That just makes more obvious what's happened to you. *It's become an act.* Even that matchstick you keep chewing on has become a gimmick, part of your image. Gawd, how I wish that word had never been made up! Damn all images to hell!" The protest was so vehement that Cousin Clem guiltily removed the matchstick from between his teeth and thrust it into his pocket, slinking away a step or two as he did. "Now I want this stopped. You go back to the way you were — 'Them nude self-portraits of hers have put her behind in her work,' that's the ticket — or I'll have to conclude that you don't have it any more. You're washed up. I mean that, Clem. One more 'successfully disinfected of subject matter' or 'countervailing modalities' and it's curtains. Closing time. Walking papers. Bye bye, blackbird."

Slocum dropped into his swivel chair breathing heavily, and waved both Clem and me off before there could be any resumption of the nervous strain against which his doctor had warned him. Clem shuffled out of the office and down the two flights of stairs into the street, followed by his faithful old hound dog, Rip, another prop in which Slocum was beginning to lose his faith.

◎◎◎

In an all-out effort to recover the bucolic flavor that had made him a true primitive, and that I must agree had been slipping away from him, Clem moved out of the house with its flourishing urbanity, now seen as one source of contamination, and into the barn. There instead of the volumes on art in which he had been steeping himself in the misguided quest for broadened horizons, he now did faithfully again read the *Wallaces Farmer* he had begun his career pretending to work for, back copies of which had been piling up on the porch (neglected by more than himself, if it came to that). He had a portable transistor radio which he kept tuned to country music at all times, even when driving the tractor or engaged upon the other duties into which he plunged with renewed industry once again. His lunch he ate in the fields or under a tree, sucking at a jug of cold cider swung about on the side of his arm, in keeping with folk tradition. Now and then a can of Schlitz, opened half an hour before mealtime to let it breathe for a bit. He gave an especially wide berth to Charlie Achorn, whose conversation also ran to reminiscences of artists he had met or befriended in his time, men like Arp and Miró and Giacometti, personal impressions often accompanied by finely honed comments on their work such as would gravely retard Clem's rehabilitation. Dinner like as not he took in town, reverting even there to the overalls and bandannas he had begun to supplant with gabardine suits and porkpie hats, and trailed ever by the old hound dog he had let adopt him.

Then came mounting tension as the time approached for his next *Bugle* review. Slocum took it gingerly when it was handed him. Again on deck as mentor, I knew what the copy said — and that it would probably prove inconclusive as a test. It was a notice of an exhibition by a water colorist who was himself a primitive, so there wasn't much room for our natural to go astray in.

"Critics can enter new periods too, you know," Clem volunteered as we anxiously watched Slocum swing choppily to and fro in his chair, reading.

"It could be worse, it could be better," Slocum said when he had finished. "It's still touch-and-go. You're still on probation as far as I'm concerned. I mean is this a hick talking, with his hick intuitions? No. This is a dude, a city slicker conning us out of our brains. Do you want to be a city slicker?"

"No sirree, Bob!" Clem said, kneading his cap in both hands with absolute bumpkin authenticity.

"Are you going to give us back that hayseed? That rube on whose foxy insights we can ever rely?"

"Yes sirree, Bob! Just you watch. I'll knock that prose style o' mine back down to where she belongs. I'll knock it looser'n a busted bellyband!"

The trouble was that the next two shows coming up, which Clem was to combine in one review, were by artists belonging to a new school who called themselves the Centrifugalists. A variant of Op Art *redivivus* (as poor Clem could hardly avoid pointing out), it aimed at optical effects whirling the viewer's eye off into space, as befit the concept of an expanding universe from which its adherents took inspiration. The first artist, Kunigunde Smith, put the canvas around the frame as a guarantee that the work would have no center, further implementing her purpose by having the canvas revolve.

Srnecz went a step further. He worked in disagreeable conformations and nauseating color combinations aimed at making viewers avert their eyes from the canvas, while being further distracted by rain falling on them at unpredictable intervals from ceiling pipes fitted with a spigot secretly manipulated by the artist. His purpose was to drive people out of the gallery altogether, and not merely away from pictures threatening to imprison their vision within arrangements of paint and fabric and other inherently parochial materials.

"This is the most iconoclastic anti-art we have seen since the Dadaists first subjected the public to cacophonical noises and incoherent gibberish, when not insulting or physically assaulting them on the streets of Paris," one critic was quoted in the catalogue as saying. "Events such as this should bring that much closer to realization the hope expressed by Marcel Duchamp in a letter to Alfred Steiglitz, that people would come to despise painting."

It was impossible not to deal with this on the highest intellectual level, and Clem strove to muffle what must be said in all the colloquialisms at his command. And Ed Slocum read with visible relief the opening paragraph of the copy handed him, doing so as he rounded his desk to sit down. "Well, take this dollar bill, hotfoot it down to the corner drugstore and fetch me some Dramamine if it ain't the Centrifugalists come to town," it began.

Slocum looked up with a smile, and nodded at his critic.

"Kinda like it though," it continued. "Kinda cotton to it, must say. Stuff's a trip all right." And so on. Then Slocum's eye ran into stuff like "kinetic equilibrium," "linear spasms," "coagulated space," and "defecated inheritances."

When Slocum had read clear through to the end, he set the manuscript down on his desk, and, pushing his glasses up onto his forehead, rubbed his eyes with his fingertips.

"It's brilliant of course. Superb. You're fired."

"How'd you like that part about planting its flag plumb in that Void where art don't amount to a hill of beans?" Clem said, bearing a momentarily weird resemblance to Walter Brennan. "That homespun? That earthy?"

"Yeah, like" — Slocum singled out an especially exquisite

phrase — "'the apocalyptic distillation of contemporary Angst you can bet your sweet ass.'"

"There's still primitive in that."

"Two percent. The rest is all that guck." Slocum rose and slowly navigated the room, his hands deep in the hind pockets of his trousers. "If it was just me, that'd be one thing. I'd take it into consideration. But as you know yourself, papers have been cancelling out of the syndicate right and left. Only three more left out of the dozen or so, besides the *Bugle*, and they'll bow out when they get a load of" — Slocum bent around to glance at the copy again — "'herniated cubism.' No, it's too late." He sighed heavily. "You've gone and made a damn silk purse out of the sow's ear I hired. We can't recover the natural you once were. We cannot fish the apple back out of the strudel, the egg from the omelet. This is it, Clem. A genuine natural is hard to find, and believe me, harder to lose. But this is curtains," Slocum said, and his tone and aspect became oddly like that of a gangster as he stood once more behind his desk and said across it: "You know too much."

COUSIN CLEM WENT INTO AN EMOTIONAL SLUMP AS PROFOUND
as it was prolonged. Suspended between two irreconcilable
personae, he no longer knew who he was, yokel or intellectual, primitive or sophisticate, farmhand or journalist.
Or he was in each case both, and being both, neither. Not
fit to resume the tasks of hired man thanks to the headier
station he had briefly tasted; yet unable to imagine what
else he might undertake that would be more congenial to
his ego as altered — while fear of failing at whatever that
might be kept him from even looking. He lay about the
barn, and then the house into which the others at last bod-
ily carried him, in a funk that was a kind of limbo, from
which none could guess when he might emerge, if ever. I
was disturbed in a bag lunch at my desk by another of
those mother-and-daughter telephone calls, urging that I
hurry with all possible speed to Pretty Pass.

"You've been a beacon guiding us through troubled
waters —" the mother began on one extension.

"Now you've got a catatonic on your hands," said the

daughter on the other. "And your patient is sinking fast."

The designation given, rather than that of "client," caused me a twinge of apprehension as to what I was now considered to be practicing. I was glad that I had so far refused all payment. I flew to the farm, springing out of my car to find Hattie waiting for me at the door.

"I hope you've got some good ideas up your sleeve this time, *Doctor* Bumpers."

"Where is he?"

Clem was stretched out on a parlor sofa, his eyes fixed in a dull glaze on the ceiling, a bowl of chicken soup untouched at his elbow, old Rip the hound dog "failing" at his feet in sympathy. Heck and Charlie Achorn were also on deck, and so we stood four-strong gazing down at the prostrate figure, as at the remains of one in the last stages of willed self-termination. Of that diagnosis I was immediately sure.

"Another identity crisis," I murmured, remembering Mother Sigafoos's remark that there was "a lot of that going around," an observation certainly borne out by glimpses of farmers who didn't know who they were leaning on neglected fences between which one tooled by on dusty backroads, smoking pipes or chewing blades of barley grass as they stared into space.

"Pirandello —" Charlie Achorn began, and was seized by the arm and marched forcibly out of the room by Heck Brown.

Not that he need have bothered. Clem no longer gave a damn what anybody said, within earshot or out, and he couldn't have cared less whether Achorn had been about to launch an analysis of his, Clem's, predicament as that of a character in a drama of molten selves, or offer up some anecdotal tidbit about the Italian genius. Clem not responding to any of my questions, preferring to remain in the kind of catatonic stupor we call "elective," Hattie and I joined the other two — leaving the bowl of chicken soup on the table for the dog to scramble up and guzzle, before again jumping down to pine away with his chin on his master's shins, in a show of devotion some of us were beginning to find a trifle bogus. Put out in his kennel, he would emit long, ululating howls whenever Clem had a sinking spell. "Not yet!" Heck would yell out the window. "He can't wait to show his loyalty," Hattie would say.

Charlie Achorn shuffled off to resume work. I paced the house, thumbnail to teeth, trying to arrive at some course of action less drastic than spiriting Clem off to a sanatarium, with its enormous bills and attendant hazards of falling into the hands of some incompetent. Hattie paused at the window watching Achorn, who seemed to be standing amid the cornstalks in one of his ever-lengthening pauses in the day's occupation. "What in God's name is he doing?" she said. "Observing a moment of silent tribute to himself," said Heck who saw no reason to suspend the crackle of civilized discourse just because they had in the house and on their hands one of the worst cases of alienation on record in these parts.

I had an idea.

"Has anyone taken his temperature?"

The other two looked blankly at one another and then at me.

"Why, no," Heck said. "Why do you ask?"

"He felt kind of warm to me. Maybe he's got something."

How relieved we were to note Clem was running a fever of a hundred and three! Now we could at least call in a doctor. That was something. We could act.

"Who'll we get?" Hattie said. "Doc Perkins doesn't make house calls any longer. Nobody will."

No, Doc Perkins didn't either. But he was willing to meet a patient halfway.

"Can you get him to the Five Corners Drive-in do you think in, let me see, it's one o'clock now. Make it half an hour. I like to grab a hamburger there for lunch. Done and done."

We had some trouble up-ending the limp invalid and getting him through the front door, holding his arms while his toes grazed the threshold, and out to the Browns' car, into the back seat of which we finally managed to wedge him. I rode there too, along with the dog, who sprang in for the auto ride on which he was always keen, thrusting his nose out the partly opened window to sniff the breeze. Clem continued silent for most of the trip, neither cooperating nor resisting. Then suddenly he began to jabber. "Chromatic subtlety," he said. The words seemed to have been jarred out of him by a bump in the road. Then it was like a bung drawn from a barrel. "Post-abstractionist contrapuntality. Regurgitated Fauvism."

"He's delirious," Hattie said to Heck, who was driving.

Doc was waiting for us at the hamburg drive-in. He promptly got out of his car and joined us in ours, clutching his bag. I drew Clem over to make room for us all in the back seat, sweeping the dog to the floor.

"Here comes a waitress," the doctor said. "Let's get our orders in first. What does everyone want?"

A girl in a polka dot diaper and string bra churned across the intervening gravel, drawing a pencil from her hair and popping her gum with aristocratic *hauteur.*

"What'll you have, Clem?"

"Fragmented simultaneities. Conceptualized deliquescences."

The upshot of it was that we ordered five whopperburgers with the works and five Cokes, deciding for Clem in the hopes of finally "getting something into him," as Doc Perkins put it, digging into his bag.

"Now then, what seems to be the trouble, Clem?"

"Spatial dilapidation. Conglomerated perspective."

"I see. Anything else?"

"Pictorial carnage. Eviscerated verisimilitudes."

"Christ. I've never run into anything like this before. Anything else?"

"Countervailing polytonalities. Solipsistic de-quantifications."

"I don't know anything about art, but I know this man is sick. Let's see about your temperature."

A thermometer poked into Clem's mouth confirmed the reading recently taken. Doc drew a tongue depressor from his bag. "Now then, let's take a look at that throat. Stick your tongue out. Not that way. *For* me, not *at* me. Mmm . . . Angry hatch all right. Probably strep. No end of that going around. That tongue is no bargain either. What are all those little papules on it?"

"Sprackled longitudinalities. Visual pandemonium."

"You're telling me. That dog's tongue is no prize either. Could somebody do something about him?" The

Browns between them hauled Rip over into the front seat where he could not interfere with the examination — which now consisted in Doc's stalking Clem's chest with the bell of the stethoscope. "Let's just unbutton your shirt ... Hmm ... Little music in there. Don't hear it playing 'When the Roll Is Called up Yonder' though. No, it's mainly the strep throat. I'll just take a culture —"

"Sub-bourgeois counter-culture."

"— and send it to the lab, but I know it's positive. I'll prescribe an antibiotic that should clear it up in three or four days. Ah, here are our whopperburgers."

"What about the insomnia?" Heck asked.

"Good night's sleep will fix that up. Never saw it to fail."

◉◉◉

The problem by no means disappeared with the strep infection. The self-sabotage on which Clem was internally bent went on after that was cleared up. His strength continued to ebb with his spirit. He declined nourishment, the more swiftly to accomplish his end. That seemed near. Then there was a sudden revival of energy accompanied by a return of color to his cheeks, a definite brightening of the eye. But Mrs. Sigafoos dashed the hopes briefly roused by that turn for the better. "It's the death glow," she said, using the famous old wives' term for the flush that often precedes departure. "It'll probably be some time tonight, or early tomorrow morning." Outside in his kennel, Rip was tuning up.

That baleful prediction hardly came true. My own personal belief, that Clem would linger on indefinitely, half of him clinging to the life from which the other half wished to exit, was indeed borne out. That gave me time to think, and think hard, about our central problem, now at least thoroughly defined, brought to razor-edge focus: how to revive Clem Clammidge's will to live.

SALVATION CAME FROM A QUARTER I SHOULD NEVER IN A MIL-
lion years have imagined. It involved the reappearance of
an old friend whom I had first known in boyhood days in
our native Muscatine, who was later to be my roommate at
the Eastern prep school to which we were both sent, then
for a year, before he dropped out, at Demeter U. In a
quainter time, and not so long ago at that, he would have
been known as a "bad influence," with whom I had "sown
my wild oats." Nobody talks any more about sowing wild
oats in an era in which everyone is uninhibitedly rolling in
the hay. With Artie Pringle, promiscuity wasn't just a
privilege but a duty, even a kind of discipline, a challeng-
ing call to arms — anybody's — and to touch on him at all
is necessarily to relate something of my own share in the
sexual revolution with whose far-reaching reverberations I
was now professionally coping. A destiny that links Artie
Pringle and Clem Clammidge is grotesque enough; yet in
retrospect they seem to occupy their places naturally
enough in the mosaic of my own life.

I was brooding about Cousin Clem as I stood at my office window gazing abstractedly across the street at the Bijou III, where Heck and the rest of Ma Godolphin's social corona caught their Bogart Festivals and Fields revivals. There, a few months before, Artie Pringle had unexpectedly surfaced after several years in which I had lost all trace of him. *The Exorcist* was being shown then, with all the hoopla attendant on its release. I was padding in a light rain past the theatre when I stopped on a dime and did a double take on a short figure standing amid the damp throngs waiting to see the picture. He was swaddled against the worsening weather in layers of clothing by no means aiming at sartorial unity, but there was no mistaking the bright peppercorn eyes peering out through the drizzle from under a dripping pie cap.

"Artie Pringle!" I exclaimed, pausing to pump his hand. "Fancy! So you still dig this sort of thing."

"Well, that's it," Artie responded, plunging in without reciprocal greeting, and evincing no amazement at our running into each other again after years of having dropped utterly out of one another's orbit. "Dig we must if we want to avail ourselves of all, repeat, all the experiences open to man, right? As Havelock Ellis says in his introduction to *Against the Grain*, 'Therefore' " — he drew down a steaming woollen muffler through which his words had more or less up to now been filtering — " 'Therefore soak yourselves in mysticism, follow every intoxicating path to every impossible beyond, be drunk with medievalism, occultism, spiritualism, theosophy, even, if you will, Protestantism, the cup that cheers but never inebriates.' You'll admit there are things that defy rational explanation."

"Yes," I said, running an eye along the line stretching three and four abreast to the end of the block and around the corner to God knew where. "What are you doing, Artie? I did hear vaguely that you moved here after the Village. I mean Iowa, I never heard exactly where."

"I run the Midwestern branch office for Brent Caxton — the New York lecture agent? Old friend of my father's, how I fell into that. Stopgap. We'll see. Hanging loose." He shrugged. "It's not your living that matters but your life, what you dig. It's big business though, popping television stars and literary lions and aging actresses around the country and even the world. And you? I heard you were a marriage counselor or something." There seemed a faint touch of amusement at anyone's wishing to constitute himself a preservative for an institution so clearly on the skids.

"Yes. We must get together sometime, and *soon*." I had by now unobtrusively edged my way under an umbrella being grasped by a tall woman in a belted raincoat, and it was within the half-shelter of this that I conducted my end of the remainder of the meeting. For though Artie's interest in the occult as such was no news, I was loth to take my leave until I had satisfied my curiosity on one or two points regarding the current phenomenon responsible for our reunion.

"Tell me something. How come you and millions of others will go to all this trouble and hardship to see a picture that by all accounts will give you nightmares, to say nothing of making you lose your appetite for days on end? I mean you hear members of the audience get sick, right there in the theatre."

"Well, that's it. The flick is a breakthrough in that it

postulates revulsion as a legitimate objective of art. What Andy Warhol did for boredom this does for disgust. Of course the uninitiated might not grasp the point at first," he said, again with the tolerant smile remembered of old. "Yes, people woof their cookies at graphic junctures in the piece, but it's all part of the scene."

"A form of audience participation."

"You could say that."

"But then the standing around for hours on end like this rain or shine, getting on deck at dawn and whatnot, the way you do. Look how far back you are in a line you can't see the end of. You may not even get to *see* the next showing, for God's sake. You must have been here half the day already. Why do people do it?"

Again the amused pursing of the lips. "You were never wired for anything very far out, were you, Bill?" He paused to take in my jacket of conventional check, button-down shirt and tie selected with an eye to harmony. "No, the thing is, this is *itself* a cult," he explained, waving at the sopping queue. "A form of hysteria if you will, that goes with the work of art we're about to see — we *rap*. David Riesman points out — you prolly saw his in-depth analysis — that people standing around all day get to meet each other, and that way to communicate. Look how even you and I are rapping, and you not even here to catch the flick. You should. Don't be thrown by all the upchucking and the screaming, the fits, people fighting and fainting and having to be carried out feet-first — I believe there's the ambulance now. Prolly the climax, where the exorcism's in full swing. The whole thing is an experience on a gut level we all sorely need in these days of superficial relationships and facsimile connections. Why should I have to explain all this to you — and you a psychologist. You should above all understand it," he finished with another wave at the crowd. "How it bespeaks a passionate involvement. It shows people are committed."

"Or should be."

"Well, that's it. Let's don't be so timid about what we expect out of art. 'Paint me the bold anfractuous rocks/ Faced by the snarled and yelping sea.' So don't be turned off by the communal barfing and the shrieks and howls and one thing and another. That bespeaks a — need I spell it out? — bourgeois turn of mind." Artie lapsed once more into good-natured amusement, getting his chops up over my threads. "I mean that's not where it's at. That's two-dimensional Dripsville. That's" — his voice dropped to a pitying whisper — "our old scoutmaster."

A last curiosity remained to be satisfied before I must gallop away on business of my own. One had heard reports and caught wisps of rumor about Artie's life-style.

"I suppose, Artie, you're, well, I mean *into* a lot of these things in fact as well as theory?"

"Oh, sure. I'm moving with a fast crowd, yes — though I wish this one would get shuffling. I've got a lecture on diabolism to catch after the show, and then tonight it's the usual séance at Madame Baklava's. We get in touch with departed spirits at her pad on Saturday nights. Ask whether they're adjusting to death and that sort of thing. Last week we tried for hours to communicate with Max Ernst — for my money the best of the whole surrealist lot. But it was a clinker. Nothing. Zero."

"Max Ernst is still alive."

"Well, then that explains it. Because Madame Baklava rarely draws a bummer. Lets the group pick its choice by majority vote. What a legend in his lifetime Ernst must be that we could pull a booboo like that! Tonight we'll be sure it's somebody who's actually crossed over into camp ground."

"That would help."

He now eyed me with a less caustic speculation.

"You might be a help. Care to sit in sometime?"

"Oh, sure. For a long time I've thought I'd like to dabble in that — things best kept from mortal men and so on. Are you in the book? I'll give you a ring."

"Sure, or you can reach me during the day at the Caxton office. I'm the whole staff, except for a secretary. Maybe I'll give you a clang. Ah, the old ark's a-moverin'. Toodle-oo."

"Bye, Artie."

Musing — to the extent to which it can be called that when one is in full trot — on Artie Pringle's immersion in the occult, I wondered to that day whether he knew what I knew about the disaster in which it had once landed him. It had brought to an end, or at least a momentary halt, his hopes for some kind of literary career. Writing had not been an ambition, but on financial backing from his father he had founded a magazine called *Gargoyle*, one of those periodicals that never get beyond Volume I Number 1, usually for eventual lack of funds. The reason in this case was different. Artie had filled the entire first issue of *Gargoyle* with five stories submitted by a writer he hailed in its opening pages as a sensational discovery of his own, the greatest practitioner of the exotic since Huysmans. There was no second issue because it would have been filled with letters pointing out that the touted stories were to be found in a collection known as *Les Diaboliques* by a nineteenth-century French writer named Barbey d'Aurevilly. Artie had been had by a twentieth-century hoaxter in Peoria, Illinois. What had made it so especially excruciating was its being perpetrated in a field professed to be Artie's own. Was that why he had fled the Village laughter and buried himself back here, at least until gleeful intellectuals might be hoped to have forgotten the incident, or time to have dimmed its memory?

⊚⊚⊚

I couldn't get Artie out of my mind, in the days following the encounter at the Bijou III. Despite his *outré* viewpoint — or perhaps because of it — he had always retained my fascination. At the very least I was itching to know what he finally thought of the picture. So I rang him up and asked just that.

"Oh, we never did get to see it. Yet, I mean."

" 'We'?"

"Yes. Right after you left I started rapping with this chick nearby in the line? She overheard some of your comments — well, never mind that. So after a couple more hours we both suddenly realized we were famished, so I suggested we split and grab a bite to eat and then come back later and get in line again. That's done a lot with *The Exorcist*, you know. Part of the whole scene. So we scarfed up a few skeins of spaghetti in that Italian restaurant there, along with a bottle of Chianti which needless to say facilitated this fast-ripening friendship. Then we backtracked to the theatre with our tickets — to find *kabloom*. God knows what the scene was inside but the riot squad was outside and the manager was cancelling the performance. Half in hysterics himself."

"That was tough. What did you do then?"

"Threw up our hands and came over here to my place. Agatha's still here. I mean it looks like a thing, within the usual limits of everybody hanging loose. Like to make a foursome of it Saturday? She likes your profile, and as for me, well, you're just my height, if you can call it that. Can you find some quail in the little black book?"

"It's been slow, Artie."

"Agatha's got a friend. A dozen in fact. Want to meet us here at seven, say, taking potluck on the companion?"

"Sure."

The evening itself was of no great importance in my life except insofar as it conducted me back once more into Artie's orbit, with all that that implied about him as a "bad influence," part of a fast crowd rumored to indulge in regular orgies and whatnot. My date was a pleasant enough girl named Susan Martin who, in the course of our quadrilateral dinner at the same Italian spaghetti house, made it clear that she had no taste for group sex, though not being straitlaced when it came to the Pair as designed by nature. "I don't suppose you're wired for that sort of thing either, eh, Bill?" Artie said. I made some ambiguous reply intended to indicate neither a libertine nor a bluenosed approach to such matters, but it was Susan who kept in the thick of the argument, with telling results. "Look, Artie," she said, "you talk away about a permissive society, but it isn't permissive at all." He looked at her blankly across his wineglass. "A girl isn't *allowed* to do these things, she's

expected to. So it isn't permissiveness, it's just the reverse
— compulsory." "Touché!" I said, a response that may or
may not have been instrumental in netting me Susan's
company for the night.

Artie was visibly needled by the thrust. He was silent,
hostilely so, until a little more wine and then a few records
back at his pad thawed him out once again and made him
quite forget the battle of wits in which he'd been bested by
a woman. At one point, he beckoned me into the kitchen
with a jerk of his head. It was just to say that an orgy had
in fact been slated for two weeks from Saturday, here in his
place. Agatha would not be among those present, since she
was heading out for the Coast in a few days, so the participants would all be new to me except for Artie.

"It's all lined up with the usual bunch, so you don't even
have to bring a chick. But bring some wine or a casserole or
something if you cook, because we all chip in on that. The
rest is, you know, potluck again."

⊚⊚⊚

What I seem to remember most about the orgy is how
the Pilgrim fathers kept running incongruously through my
head during nearly the whole of it. It was very odd, and
more than a little unnerving. The explanation that will
spring immediately to your mind, of course, is that here is a
plain case of bad conscience, the ingrained Puritan heritage laying its damp hand on yet another supposedly
emancipated American youth. As though the ghost of Governor Bradford himself hovered over our revels saying, "So
this is the new morality, and these are *its* pioneers." That

may have been true as far as it went, but it was only part of the story.

Of all my schoolday studies of the *Mayflower* and Plymouth Colony, Thanksgiving and the Indians and the rest, the incident that stands out most vividly in my recollection concerns the diplomatic visit paid Massasoit, one time, by a Pilgrim delegation consisting of Edward Winslow, Stephen Hopkins, and the indispensable Squanto, the ticklish purpose of which was to get the Chief to get his subjects for God's sake to stop sponging food and drink at the settlement, where things were hard enough without a constant stream of redskins who had adopted the charming New England custom of dropping in simply in order to freeload. Massasoit gracefully agreed, and then showed what *he* was capable of in the way of hospitality. Nothing would do but that the entire delegation spend the night in bed with himself and his squaw, making thereby a party of five presently expanded to seven when two more Wampanoag braves piled in with them and started to sing, what was more; so that, as Winslow later described it in his memoirs, "we were worse weary of our lodging than of our journey" — my personal nomination for the best one-liner in American literature.

So it wasn't conscience as much as congestion that accounted for my nagging historical association. We, too, were seven in one bed, at least a lot of the time. The party was as mixed a bag as could be wished in an enterprise of this sort. But the most formidable entry by far was a lady wrestler, or former lady wrestler, named Stella ("Muscles") Marinière. The nickname was obviously the concoc-

tion of some promoter or press agent, though Artie insisted
that her last name very closely approximated what it had
been tinkered into by the box-office-minded colleague. "I
think Marinera, or something like that. Because she is Italian." Her athletic years were over now. But her behavior in
bed was an obvious determination to relive her great days
in the ring, and only a lurking male death wish could
account for her continuing supply of sparring partners.

Being locked in a priapic clasp with Muscles Marinière
was like being entangled in a nest of boa constrictors. Four
in all, functioning in pairs. I was sure her embrace alone
would finish me off by caving in my torso, leaving my ribs
in splinters. Then when in each of her innumerable crises
she wrapped both legs around my back, I was convinced
this was it spine-wise. It would be snapped cleanly in two
like a stick of kindling, while a hammerlock would add its
share to the general skeletal debris. My own exertions
ended in a sort of death rattle as I rolled off the Amazon
onto the bed, where I lay gasping into the pillow like a
beached fish — or a Laocoön saying "Uncle." A gingerly
tally of my bones revealing after all no breaks or fractures,
either compound or simple, I rested a bit, whimpering as I
smoked a cigarette.

My next engagement was a tripartite skirmish with a sex
kitten who liked to scratch, and a tall blonde given to bit-
ing her prey. As the one executed a little scrimshaw work
on my hide while the other cannibalized the unoccupied
portions of me, I wondered whether my Blue Cross insurance was in order. I had been in a period of grace with it.
At last the Etcher lay back and said, "I've been a very, very

naughty girl. Now aren't you going to give me a tongue lashing?" Thus Artie Pringle's boast that we were "a highly decadent little click" was not idle, though this debauchee failed the taste test when, a divertimento known as sixty-nine being proposed, he demurred, though adding assurances that he would not be averse to a little thirty-four-and-a-half. Thereby casting a momentary pall over the proceedings, and serious doubt whether he was going to fit in with the bunch. The fourth woman was a plump redhead of thirty or so, who kept swooning like a lady of quality. The only other man besides Artie and me was the owner of a Volvo agency named Harry Doberman who, though oldest, was the most impressive gymnast. Unmarried, this magnifico was said to seek in quenchless lust a solace for being unable to love. Artie, who had forearmed me with a brief dossier on each of the participants, had reflected longest over Doberman, pulling his underlip in thought before saying, "He likes women, and he likes men, but he doesn't like anybody."

The operating principle of such sexual smorgasbords of course is to improvise without inhibition and as fancy dictates. It resulted in some extraordinary juxtapositions. At one point I found somebody's foot in my mouth just as I aspired to a dimly discernible globed breast, the mate of which was busy at the moment. It was in the first gray light of dawn, while crawling among the charred remains of my companions looking for a place to get some sleep, that the parallel with Massasoit's slumber party struck most forcibly home. The same sense of shared hardships, of consumed energies and consuming fatigue, will similarly overtake your sexual pioneer — if we may borrow the term imagined as having been ironically dropped by the shade of Governor Bradford on those shenanigans of one's salad days.

Our indulgences had naturally been supplemented with drink, and a few of us popped back pellets of a mildly hallucinogenic sort, so that at one point (in lieu of more graphic visitations) the actor Edward Everett Horton seemed suddenly to have penetrated our midst, clucking and poking among the shambles and doing the famous double and triple takes as he dithered, "Oh, my word, this is — Oh, goodness me, such — And this, my, my. I declare never in all my born days . . ." Perhaps there was some associative thread linking him in my mind with the clergyman Edward Everett Hale, despatching a possible collateral descendant to scold us. I don't know.

Come mid-morning, I picked my way out of bed, rousing Muscles Marinière, who began a taunting recital of my limitations as noticed in the course of the saturnalia. "You know what you are? A prude!" I continued primly on to the bathroom for which I was bound. "You're vanilla! Strictly vanilla." I gained my retreat and quickly locked the door behind me. "I'm coming in there with you!"

I examined myself queasily in the medicine-chest mirror. My eyes were bloodshot — they looked like gnawed cherry pits — my tongue had turned as suspected into a thick slice of mold cheese, while my chest and shoulders looked as though I had spent the night running naked through bramble patches. Someone had gnawed a small hole in the mustache I was trying to grow. It was a poor thing at best, probably no more than Alice B. Toklas's, if Dad's memories of Paris could be trusted.

I splashed my face with cold water, and managed on rubber legs to reach the kitchen, where thank God I saw an electric percolator full of coffee. I was sitting at the table with a hot mug of that, wearing shorts and a shirt I had snatched up on my way out of the bedroom, when I heard someone enter behind me. Giving my back a quarter-turn brought the Etcher into view, knotting up the sash of a flowered wrapper.

"Good morning," I said. "And how do you feel?"

"Like hammered garbage."

"You have such a way with words. As Pope said, 'What oft was thought, but ne'er so well express'd.' "

"Screw you."

"Marry me."

"And screw the Pope. You Catholic?" she asked with her head in the icebox.

"Only in my taste. And pray let no such barrier come between us. Oh, I know I presume when I ask for your hand in that most sacred of bonds, but let that presumption be a gauge of the love that spurs my humble petition. I know, too, I should first have sought an audience with your father, hoping thus to forearm my poor plea with his blessing, but may you find it within your maidenly charity to let this breach of amenity too be but another measure of my ardor — an ardor I shall invite all the vicissitudes of life to test, to my last mortal breath as the husband of your bosom."

"I said to piss off."

"Not till I have poured out my heart — a vessel of whose contents I have emptied but the half — the tenth — the hundredth! Oh, my angel, my —"

"Oh, my ass, will you? Have you got the cream there?"

"Yes. And may this small service," I continued, pouring a dollop into her coffee from the carton on the table, "be an earnest of the numberless daily devotionals by which I pledge to prove myself worthy of that affirmative answer I yearn now to hear from one I have worshipped too long from afar." Here I sank to my knees in front of her chair and, parting the skirt of her robe, began to swirl my tongue around in her navel. "I shall declare my feelings to your father. I shall go so far as to seek the good offices of your mother in my cause ere I seek the favor of his answer. Only speak to me now! Do I live or die?"

"Why do you talk like a creep?"

"I have this vocabulary problem," I said, rising and returning to my own chair, "which, give me leave to hope, will not hinder my cause. Oh, let not these sentiments, too long suppressed, fall on stony ground for want of better than the paltry speech in which I must so pitifully couch them. Not, believe me my archangel, that any words could begin to do them justice."

"Knock off the *Wuthering Heights* bit, how about it. Because I know it's Jane Austen." She stirred her coffee a moment, musing. "Christ, they actually used to talk that way once. Do you realize that?" She gave a slight shudder. "That must have been a drag."

I was breathing heavily from my recitative, the Etcher across from me clawing the rind from an orange whilst stating that her mouth tasted like the bottom of a bird cage, when Muscles joined us, swinging her arms heartily, as though spoiling to get a half-Nelson on another combatant.

"That Artie. Wanting to make love again when he knows it's too soon."

I must contribute an aphorism: after all, I had neglected to bake a cake or bring a casserole.

"Ah, yes," I began, holding my splitting head in both hands as I groped blindly toward an absolute. "Orgies, my dear Muscles, orgies are like space travel. There is always the problem of re-entry."

"Well, if it isn't Vanilla." She had evidently settled on this nickname for me as one emphasizing my limits as an erotic partner, or rather my restrictions in taste: adherence to the rudimentary in face of all the other twenty-seven flavors available. "He can sure keep the conversational ball rolling though. Hear him clear through the house," she added, tweaking my ear as she continued on to the refrigerator. "Say something, Vanilla. Something cultural."

"Well, I might recall, apropos that charming little habit of yours, that Gandhi, too, was given to tweaking people's ears. I just give you that, Muscles," I said, wondering as I did so whether my own mightn't eventually cauliflower as a result of return engagements with Muscles.

Fruit juices were poured, bacon and eggs fried, boxes of cereals foraged for as the others straggled in. Most looked like death warmed over. To get the party back out of the doldrums into which it threatened to fade, people began trading limericks and other forms of racy verse. When all else had contributed, Muscles said, "Hey, Vanilla hasn't been heard from yet. Know any poems, Vanilla? Come on, give us a ditty."

"All right," I said, and rose and rapidly recited: "My

father calls me William, my mother calls me Will, my sister calls me Willie, but the fellows call me Bill."

"And you said 'Yessum' to your teacher."

"No'm, I never said 'Yessum.'"

Glances conveyed the generally crystallizing view that I was a bacchanalia-poop, and the suspicion that this was probably the last moist heap to which I would be asked. But there followed a round of gamey stories to which I was able to contribute one or two entries of a mildly lubricious sort, enough once again to loose Edward Everett Horton's phantom dithering and clucking about the premises, "Oh, dear me, such — Bless my soul, did you hear what he just — Great Scott, I never in all my born — Oh, just listen to them, who knows what they're coming to . . ."

◎◎◎

I was still standing at the office window long after the workman had finished with the marquee and dragged his ladder off again, smiling to myself at the memory. I wondered what had happened to Artie and all the gang — and why neither of us had called the other again since, or made any effort to keep in touch. I would correct that right away. I phoned his office straight off, and was put through to him by a secretary-receptionist with the gentlest, most musical voice I had ever heard. It was so like tinkling bells that, having made a lunch date with Artie for the next day, I told him that I'd be only too glad to pick him up at his office. I must see Miss Dulcet.

God (to fall back on the old Portuguese proverb) never wrote straighter with crookeder lines. More than one destiny hung in the balance as I shot up the elevator to Artie's office, though I little dreamed it at the time. The girl at her post in the tiny outer office quite matched the voice as remembered. A soft ash blonde with large gray eyes and a clear amber skin, and to have her speak your name was like hearing it for the first time, to actually feel the word flowing like a melodious current down your spine to your very loins. It was like a touch of her hand. Artie emerged from his private office too promptly for me to even begin trying to make hay.

"Hello, Bill. This is my friend Bill Bumpers. Miss de Lune."

I think you could say that mentally — and here I mean the speed of fantasy-ignited associations rather than logically constituted thoughts — I have what garage mechanics call in the case of automobiles a fast idle. By the time Artie and I had reached the street, I had already been married to the girl for ten years, having dined with her that very night, declared myself smitten with the first of the wine, swept her into reciprocal avowal with the opening strains of our first waltz, held her panting in my arms, drunk with her scent and mad with passion, a passion yet held in abeyance that it might all the more sweetly explode in some Caribbean bridal suite, to which we should return on each succeeding anniversary thereafter to hear the same plucked instruments, drink the same champagne and sleep in the same bed, the identical bower in which the first of our babies had surely been conceived. Bed! bed! Whispers amid cool sheets bearing by morning her blessed spoor, a nest fragrant with her own true spice. Oh, the bliss of each dawn's awakening, in a veritable heaven after all the years of Paradise Mislaid. In the selfsame bed would be contrived the delirious trysting of her seed with mine, not alone for one, but all three of the plumply perfect laughingly delightful Dresden cherubs who would make complete a life lived in total harmony and unabating prosperity — that prosperity to be guaranteed by the skill with which I could persuade the numberless couples seeking my counsel to relinquish the romantic dreams of their youth.

"How do you like my secretary?"

"Not bad. How long have you had her?"

"Only a few weeks. Just breaking her in."

"Is she . . . ?"

"No. None of that for her. Has a boy friend. But I gather it's pretty rickety. She's an actress, or an aspiring one. Only working to save enough money to take some more courses. Hopeless profession. We have two actors on our list now, top stars I mean, who've had to take to the lecture circuit to keep body and soul together. Haven't had a decent part in years. I'm here as a sort of halfway point as they're popped around the country from New York. Meeting their planes and fussing over them, seeing they're shuttled around in some kind of style though we all know except them that it's all over. Making restaurant and hotel reservations, getting maitre d's to bow from the waist a little for Christ's sweet sake."

"An actress." I was into the *déjà vu* before I even asked the question. "Miss de Lune. What's her first name?" Already bracing myself.

"Claire."

There was a rumble in my head as my amassed dreams slid like a load of shale out of a dump truck. "I see. Claire de Lune. Has she got the same press agent as Muscles Marinière?"

"No, as a matter of fact that's the funny part of it. It's her real name. The family is de Lune — from Provence I think — and her parents thought it would be cute to christen her Claire. So pin it on them. Though again the crazy part of it is that it fits her, don't you think? I mean there is something diaphanous about her, like moonlight. Her friends call her Misty. Where would you like to lunch?"

"I need a big fat martini of the kind they serve at Ma Peckinpaugh's. How would that suit you?"

"Dynamite. And then a good plate of their chicken and dumplings sounds just what the doctor also ordered."

Ma's was crowded, and there being a wait of a few minutes for a table, we wedged ourselves in at the bar. I sat next to a man on the end stool who was just then listening to the bartender, to whom he had evidently been pouring out his troubles in keeping with tradition.

"What you must remember about misanthropes," the bartender was explaining, "is that they're often also very gregarious. It seems to be the paradox of your nature that you're unable to resist invitations to parties you know you're going to break up, to seek the company of people you know you're going to insult after a few drinks. That's when the worms come out of the woodwork. Me, I stay home. But that's when you unleash all the hostilities pent up toward others, out of a sense of your own inferiority. I see it here all the time when I'm working nights. Your societal drives, then, become perversely welcome opportunities for unloading on others the insecurity you feel within yourself. You have poor ego boundaries."

The customer nodded, and buried his face in his hands in an agony of shame.

"Well, what'll you boys have?"

As over our martinis Artie and I brought one another up to date on what we'd been doing, what gossip we knew, and so on, I found myself drawn to a group at a large corner table. The main object of my attention was a woman seated there in obvious regal priority, one with the most elegant posture — I mean she carried herself *sitting* — who was dressed in the nostalgic down-home style already noted as a feature of the landscape. In the costume one wouldn't bother even trying to guess her age. Once, her dark eyes caught like burrs on my own browsing gaze, and she held my stare and returned it, till I retreated in embarrassment.

"Is that Ma Peckinpaugh over there?" I asked the bartender as covertly as I could.

He glanced over, craning his neck.

"No, that's Ma Godolphin. With her satellites."

Heck wasn't among them. I hoped that meant a return to his senses and his responsibilities at the farm, including continued solicitude for Clem. Now, I had all along had a nagging hunch about a solution for Clem's problem. It had something to do with Artie, I wasn't sure what. The idea was like the click you hear in a clock when the hands reach the moment for which the alarm is set, but the alarm isn't on. It's off, and the moment passes. Each time, I heard the subconscious click, but failed to grasp the connection. Now suddenly the bell went off. Artie had been talking about one of his stars, and that did it.

"Artie, I've got a swell client for you." He was all ears.

"You know the art critic Clem Clammidge? Cousin Clem?"

"You mean that hayseed columnist?"

"The same. You shoot him around the country, me boyo, and you'll both clean up."

"For Christ's sake, Bill, I can't book a cornball like that. Do you know what our list is like? We've got the classiest stable of any lecture agency — Look." Here he began to reel off his roster of novelists, women's lib disputants, beautiful people and other dazzlers. I cut him off with an impatient gesture.

"That just means you need a variation, and here I take your term 'stable' to heart. His platform presence alone — I mean he'll be a sensation the moment he shuffles onstage. 'Fella's derivative of we all know who, but what have you got Toulouse, Lautrec.'" Artie put his head in his hands, like the wretch on my left, and mentioned the Nazarene. "Never mind. The women's clubs will eat it up, and with reason. He represents the inverted intellectualism we all so sorely need in these parlous times, as we wind our way steadily up the semantic Tower of Babel from which the Lord God of Hosts will at last disperse us to our separate and misbegotten tongues, if he hasn't already. Cast him against type, as they say in the theatre, that's the ticket. And you, Artie, I see as the stormy petrel among impresarios —"

"Your table is ready, gentlemen."

Artie was still shaking his head as we made for it, but by the time we were seated I had made my very hard moral decision. This is what was cooking in my busy little noddle.

Politicians are said to have among them an unwritten law that goes roughly like this. You have something "on," say, a fellow member of Congress whose vote you need for a bill on which you have your heart set, or from whom you want to exact a favor. The quid pro quo is his compliance in return for your silence about the particular event in his past he wants to keep hushed up — be it a sexual indiscretion, an episode in which he has sailed too close to the wind legally speaking, or whatever. But — and here the code is iron-clad — you may use the I.O.U. only once. Once collected on, it is cancelled. You are never so much as to mention the subject again.

Central to the moral arithmetic that had gone through my head with computer speed was that here, for once, the end justified the means. I would subtly, moving crabwise, with the utmost in discreet obliquity, make clear to Artie Pringle that I had in mind the Barbey d'Aurevilly hoax with which he had begun and ended his editorial career. His secret had not to the best of my knowledge filtered this far West, to haunt him here in the breadbasket where he'd buried himself, and I would never in a thousand years have betrayed it in any case. But he didn't know that, and so as the price of my silence he might just be prevailed on to book Clem (the gruesome irony again did not escape me) into his stable of lecturers. Clem did have a certain air about him.

That decided, I resolved to bridle my tongue, bridle he says yet, until we had enjoyed some of Ma Peckinpaugh's famous chicken and dumplings, sluiced off with a stein or two of draft Heineken.

"You said over the phone you were working on a story, Artie. I know you don't like to talk about what you're writing."

"Well, that's it. The thing may evaporate in the telling. So this is an occult piece, prolly novella length, on the Faustian theme. My protagonist makes a pact with the Devil which runs that he will be given every pleasure known to mortal man on earth for twenty years, after which his soul will be claimed for damnation. So far conventional. But I think I've got a real switcheroo. When at midnight, blah blah blah, at the appointed time, all the standard ingredients, Satan is to announce what lies in store for him, the subject trembles with fear. Lakes of fire? Pits of brimstone? So run our quaking wretch's queries. Not a bit of it slyly says Mephistopheles. *Yours* will be an eternity of *pleasure* says the Dark One. What do you mean? I mean remember what you always moaned into the arms of every woman from Cleopatra and Helen of Troy down to Betty Grable? I believe, if memory serves, mmbaha ha, you employed the same cliché in describing your ecstasies — 'unbearable bliss.' A bromide, but most apt says the Dark One — who resembles Erich von Stroheim, have I told you? Well, that gave me the clue for the exquisite Hell manufactured just for you, says Satan. I condemn you to a perpetual, never-ending, eternal Orgasm. One from which there will be no respite, like I say. No says the wretch on bended knee. Not that. Yes says the Devil, giving the screw an extra quarter-turn by quoting Edwin Arlington Robinson. He recalls the line — this is the exquisite torment — about how 'hell is more than half of paradise.' Well, we'll just turn that inside out and make it 'paradise is more than half of hell.' Your orgasm, like I say, shall be unceasing. You shall writhe forever in the throes of sexual rapture.

Unbearable is good, mmbaha ha. Bursts of maniacal laughter."

Artie broke off, chewing a beaten biscuit at which he had been nervously plucking. There was a difficulty troubling him, which I thought I had divined. A slight bug in the story, one you hoped for his sake would not prove fatal.

"Of course then my Faust-type will tell the Devil he forgot one thing. 'I won't *have* another orgasm, so there, smartie. Just how will you get around that?' Whereupon I think I'll have Mephistopheles snap his fingers and cause to appear in a whirl of smoke the most divine creature that ever existed. She makes Helen of Troy look like Marie Dressler in *Tugboat Annie*. Floating toward Faust in a scented mist the siren is irresistible. Our hero's weakness is the Flesh, remember?" I nodded briskly. "He succumbs, hurling himself helplessly into one last fling before his doom — and the fling becomes the doom."

"Gee, that's great, Artie," I said, genuinely affected by the résumé, and graphically imagining the principal writhing through all eternity in a quenchless spasm of lust. "A real switch on the Faustian theme, as you say. I'd certainly be glad to publish *that* if I were an editor," I added, looking away. "Ah, here comes our food."

◉◉◉

Amply fed, indeed pleasantly glutted, we strolled back toward Artie's office, which was halfway to mine. Glances in shop windows gave back uneasy reminders of our joint want of stature, as well as ancient worries about my gait. Watching myself in a reel of home movies at a friend's place one time, I had noticed how I tended to rise up on the balls of my feet when I walked. "As though you've got a bedspring under either heel," a girl friend had later put it, troubled by the phenomenon herself. It was obviously an unconscious attempt to add with each step a fleeting inch or two to my height, but the habit was open to misinterpretation by people quick with the term "light on his feet," which I kept hearing and came to hate. So I had tried to mend my stride by cultivating a kind of duck waddle, smacking my feet down hard on the pavement with every step. We were a pair in the plate-glass reflections because of an ambulatory oddity of Artie's own. When engaged in intimate conversations of the sort he now struck up, he tended to lean confidentially toward you, with the result that, as he discoursed on details of his sex life, he kept bumping me steadily toward the curb.

"How would you like to come to another orgy?" His pronouncing the word to rhyme with "porgy" gave it a rather innocent flavor — at least seemed somehow to keep it short of absolute depravity.

"Will Muscles Marinière be there?"

"Muscles I can't promise, but I'll see what I can do."

"That won't be necessary. Anyway, I'll see."

"She's been in New York, trying to see about hitting the comeback trail I guess. But she's over the hill for that, I'm afraid." I was relieved that a return match with Muscles — what might even be a grudge fight considering our differences at the first party — did not seem in the cards. "But we've got a new quail who's really something. Like being in bed with a string of firecrackers. Know what I mean?"

"I'll see," I repeated, one foot in the gutter now.

"And I don't know whether I've ever told you about this English guy Helen sometimes brings around. He's as kinky as a telephone cord. He likes to spread marmalade on the girls, I think you dig, and then as though it's no more than crumpets with your tea —"

"I said I'd see." I heaved him firmly back toward the middle of the sidewalk with one shoulder. Strolling with Artie, one becomes like that chess piece, the bishop I think, which can only move diagonally. I must now launder this conversation by asking the question really uppermost in my mind, and my reason for hedging about group larks. "How about Claire? You say she has a steady boy friend but things are rocky?"

"Yeah. You never know with her. One day it's this, the next day that. But I've certainly given up trying to get her to join the Baredevils."

"Baredevils?"

"What we call our club. About twenty swingers in it now, and I understand it's catching on. Chapters starting all around the country. For initiation — I thought I told you all this — you have to get out on a diving board at somebody's pool and peel down to the buff with everybody watching. Then dive in. Well, here's my salt mine. Let's keep in touch."

"Just a second, Artie."

Here I must take the hard measure I had firmly decided must be taken, Machiavellian though it be.

"I'm serious about this Clem character, and I want you to think seriously about it too, or else . . ." I dropped my eyes and brushed aside a bit of non-existent sidewalk litter with the toe of my shoe.

"Or else what?"

"Or else it might get around."

"What, for Christ's sake?"

"That I've flubbed with him. His therapy. Because he's a sort of client. And I mean it would get around about me professionally. We all have things we need a friend's loyalty about — know what I mean? Things we want to keep buried in our past." I cackled hysterically, rambling on. "What do they say? A doctor can bury his mistakes, but all an architect can do is advise his clients to plant vines," I continued, wishing the ground would swallow me up.

"What in all hell . . . ?" Artie said, but he avoided my gaze in a way that made me sure the message had gone home. I grasped again at my justification: that his answer would have made no difference, that he'd already had my loyalty, I had never prattled tales out of school, and so he owed me this favor whether he knew it or not. "You mean you've got this guy in left field?"

"He's a zombie. Dead. Lazarus — and you can resurrect him. You and you alone. What do you say, Artie? Saving my client depends on his becoming yours."

"O.K. Bring him around sometime."

"Tomorrow."

10

CLEM'S REBIRTH MADE ME TASTE AS I NEVER HAD BEFORE THE exhilaration of really doing something for another human being. Because he did rise like Lazarus from the tomb at the mere mention of the idea. Tasting his first real nourishment in days, he could be seen fancying himself as I had already imagined him, shuffling onstage to drawl out the spiels pieced together from his copy before it had become spoiled. Early Cousin Clem — the vintage stuff. He was again somebody, or would be with the first crack of that autumn weather that signals the mad dispersion of authorities across the land. Artie made the recommendation over his own dead body, of course, but New York was cannier about it than he. Caxton, the agency head, stopped by on a swing of his own to the Coast, and put Clem through his preparatory paces, which the audition instantly became.

"Use the corncob pipe," he suggested, "but not too much. Kind of a prop. Light it up and maybe puff it a few times for pregnant pauses between your corkers, then set it by."

"Like Mark Twain with his cigar," Clem said. "How

about the dog?" He saw old Rip traipsing onstage at his heels, perhaps to rest at his feet while he talked, part of his aura, his mystique, but Caxton was dubious. "Too risky," he said. "Animals are always worrisome, even in plays for which they have trainers. You're afraid they'll do something wrong. No, forget the dog."

"What'll I do with him when I'm barnstorming? I can't wish him on the folks at the farm. They've got enough on their hands."

"My brother-in-law has this dog camp near here, a new thing that's caught on big. People send their dogs to camp now same as they do their children. Provide for them in every way — wholesome food, healthy group activities. Water events for spaniels and the like. Free periods in which the dogs may do what they want. Owners even get letters from camp from their pets. Once a week."

"Letters?"

"Yes. 'Dear All, I sure miss you but I'm happy here. This is a great place, it's just great. This is one keen camp, well run and everything, so don't worry about me. I was lonesome at first, but I met the most delightful bitch. Love, Bowser.' Or whatever the camp counselor cooks up. Nice touch. So have no fears about — Shep is his name?"

"Rip."

"Rip will get nothing but the best. We try to help see to it that our lecturers have nothing worrying them or preying on their minds while they're on tour. We'll have these flyers printed up and rushed to women's clubs and like organizations. So I think that does it for now. Except get cracking on those slides of the paintings you want to use. All that equipment is of course for you to supply. But an old-fashioned slide lecture once again! Oh, Bumpers mentioned about your wincing at the thirty percent fee, but that's by no means out of line for newcomers."

Of course I caught most of this in one ear as I stood in the outer reception room trying to make headway with Miss de Lune. She would lunch with me any time, but was adamant about dinner, except for the one occasion we spent an evening together, most of which was taken up with her explaining that it "would not be fair to me" if she didn't lay squarely on the line her exclusive commitment to her boy friend, one Dewey Glossop. As though impasse in that quarter were not enough, the winds blew ill again at Pretty Pass.

The inevitable happened. Charlie Achorn had done what was for him an unprecedented hitch of work, and he was itching to return once more to his cronies. Too, it was his turn again to record a batch of Dial-a-Saws. Thus, the *ménage à trois* having been returned to after a spell of quadrangular life-style, even that was in turn dissolved, leaving the farmer and his wife together once more in the old homestead. They were back to square one: again in need of a hired man. "Please, God, send us a man who wants *to farm*," Hattie said.

"If it's a praying mood you're in, why not try praying for real?" This from Mrs. Sigafoos, at whose cottage we had again converged to discuss the new crisis. "Maybe it's the old values going down the drain because people no longer go to church. I include myself in that, but I haven't been back in all these years because I couldn't bear to hear another preach in your father's pulpit. There was a man. He never interiorized none."

"There, there, Mother. All right, I'll go to church with you. Not that I quite understand how it'll solve our problem."

"Why, it's just that you may find someone among the old timers there who'll go to work. It's called the Community Church now, I believe. Our only other bet is that labor pool in town. Because I assume we don't want another shirtsleeve philosopher."

"I'd like to join you," I said, ever eager to continue my fascinated studies of a town certainly in transition. "Suppose I pick you up for the Sunday morning service. Probably eleven o'clock, but I'll check."

Owing to an unfamiliar maze of streets thrown up for a subdivision built since Mrs. Sigafoos had last been through here, she lost her bearings in giving me directions, so that when we arrived at the church the service was already in progress. The minister, a towheaded young man of thirty or so wearing a Paul Tillich sweatshirt, was just reading the Twenty-third Psalm as Charles Laughton would have done it. The congregation gave him a nice hand when he finished. Then he read some announcements, one for an open-call audition for a Beckett Festival the drama group was putting on, another having to do with the Ladies' Aid, now an encounter group. The sermon was on the subject of religious ritual as compulsive neurosis. At the end of the service, he pronounced the benediction as Jimmy Stewart would have pronounced it, which really had the worshippers in the aisles, up which they presently made their way to the strains of "Chattanooga Choo Choo," an arrangement of which the organist played as a recessional.

"I don't recognize any of these people," Mrs. Sigafoos

told us as we walked out. She was looking at the hat of a woman worshipper directly in front of us, who was saying to a companion: "It's amazing the way he keeps topping himself week after week. I don't see how he does it."

There was a brunch in the basement called Après Church, which was considered rather squarish by the more chic members of the congregation, who preferred to tool along on Bloody Marys until a combination of brunch and early dinner which they called brinner. It was they who, as it were, recongregated on the steps and sidewalk, engaging in conversations to which we listened with interest for some minutes.

"I hear Cissy's rabbit test was positive. I suppose that shoots it for college next semester?"

"Not at all. She's taking the pregnancy for her N.R.T."

"What's that?" Mrs. Sigafoos whispered to me.

"Non-resident term, I believe."

"Cissy's discussed it all with the dean, and they'll give her credit for it."

"Who's the boy?"

"Oh, it's one of those no-fault pregnancies, you know."

"Bobsy's thinking of taking her N.R.T. as a call girl. She's majoring in sociology, after all. John figures at least it will keep her off the streets."

Our little trio moved off toward my car.

"It looks as though we'll have to try the labor pool," Hattie said.

◉◉◉

So we all went down bright and early the next morning to the Acme Agricultural Employment Agency, as it was called. Threading our way slowly among the crowd of twenty-five or thirty men standing or sitting about in groups chatting, we all three found our eyes being caught by the same person. He was a lanky man in clean blue overalls and new brown work shoes. He had a rather long jaw with a trimmed beard, and he stood very erect, with one hand in his overall bib and a briar pipe in the other, nodding and talking to a couple of other men. We had not eavesdropped on him more than a minute, as he exchanged comments about the price of fertilizer and the scarcity of barbed wire ("bob wire," as it is of course always called), when we nodded to one another. Hattie stepped quickly over to a wicket behind which a young man was officiating.

"I'm interested in that man over there," she said, pointing.

"Which one is that?"

"The one who just said 'Jumping Jehoshaphat.'"

11

CLAIRE DE LUNE'S DRAWING THE LINE AT LUNCHEON FOR THE political purposes of the heart now made me take that meal alone, foregoing her inflammatory noonday company in order to spare myself the reminder that I aspired to her evening society in vain. Things seemed to have been stabilized with Dewey Glossop, bad cess to him. I even disliked breaking bread with Artie, every sight of whom made my wound throb the more.

Thus it was I found myself roosting at a local diner counter, hunched over a bowl of volcanic matter billed by the management as chili con carne. Maybe it was. Epicures of that dish leave the impression that the closer it approximates to brimstone the better. Normally I came here for the marvelous home-made apple pie, certainly the work of some unsung Ma over whose virtuosity there could be no quibble. A thickening middle having ordained a calorie limit for lunch, I was sorry I had chosen the lava, the more so because of an uneasy awareness that, as I restored my mouth with avid gulps of ice water between spoonfuls, my situation was closely followed by the counter waitress, a fetching brunette in her twenties, and not, like Miss de Lune, a couple of inches taller than the doctor ordered. She had refilled my tumbler twice already, and now leaned against some back fixtures and watched with open compassion. I humorously fanned my mouth with a hand. "Excite the membrane, when the sense has cooled, with pungent sauces."

"Multiply variety in a wilderness of mirrors."

"Well, well," I said. "You know your Eliot."

"Actually, I just read him through for a college term paper on anti-feminism in twentieth-century poetry. Eliot isn't too hard on us, except for a few things like that lampoon, 'Portrait of a Lady.' "

"Much harder on my sex. You remember Sweeney and Prufrock of course."

"Why are only females dizzy? Why are only women scatterbrained?"

"Why are only men insensitive clods? Or sterile aesthetes?"

"You're ducking the issue. Oh, you're slippery," she said with a laugh, "but I spot you for one of those people — and it's worse than open hostility — who are good-naturedly amused by women's lib."

"On the contrary, I think it's one of the seminal forces of our time." Noting this time a quiet smile, I clapped a hand to my brow. "My God, I'm always doing that! So scatterbrained. The cliché just popped out."

"Sarcasm is often like that — unconscious. So you do see us as emasculating."

"Yeah, I guess. And when you come to power you'll probably put all us male chauvinists in a penal colony. There I did it again! Where will it end! Who will save me from myself! Some more water? Keep 'em coming."

"And so is condescension often unconscious," she observed from the tap. "Like your surprise just now that I, a mere woman, had read 'Gerontion,' much less could quote it. Oh, I saw your eyebrows go up."

"No, no, it's not that at all. It was just that . . ." I sensed that I had one foot in a quagmire here, as you will have. At least I caught myself before I could say, "I meant a mere waitress." That would hardly be better. She filled the awkward pause herself.

"And as far as being treated as a sex object —"

"Oh, come, dear, not that again," I cut in, having by now a substantial store of thought on the subject to contribute. At any rate it was better than blowing on the chili. "I have often wondered if women making that particular protest aren't doing so on behalf of their, shall we say, more fortunate sisters? Those who *are* regularly whistled at? While they themselves, God forgive my saying so and present company excepted, are beating off men who aren't trying to get to them?" I grinned, adding with elephantine gallantry, "I make bold to offer the point because it conspicuously doesn't apply in your case," suicidally taking her figure in as I did. She waited with folded arms for me to administer the coup de grâce to myself. I did not fail her. Wiping my lips with what fragments remained of my disintegrated paper napkin, I cleared my throat and, gazing over her head, continued: "Doesn't it ever occur to any of you ladies

141

— of whom I hasten to add I am one of the most ardent admirers" — Oh, Christ, what grist was I not storing up for the mill of mortification through which, groaning into my pillow, I must grind myself tonight — "hasn't it ever occurred to you that if a thousand generations of maternal grandmothers hadn't been sex objects you wouldn't be here to decline the inheritance?"

"Well, this chili has certainly loosened your tongue."

"And a few teeth. I can see we have loads to talk about." Stark, staring mad, I heard myself say, "When are you through work?"

Before she could answer, I heard, like a second figment of my imagination, a voice from the back of the diner call out: "Paging Doctor Bumpers! Is there a Doctor Bumpers here? Paging Doctor Bumpers!"

Is being paged in a greasy spoon as low as you can sink, or as high as you can go? One would like to think his habits as a man about town were so generally known as to include even where he slummed. That would be charming. Two knew of one's predilection for the apple pie served here. One was Artie Pringle. The other was Hattie Brown.

All eyes were fixed upon him as he rose and made his way to the back where, next to the Gents' bog, the receiver still swayed on the cord from which it dangled. Since it was a wall phone without a booth, large and attentive was his audience as he put the receiver to his ear. It included the kitchen factotum who had paged him and who now, in his undershirt and wearing a sweatband around his neck, watched and listened through the serving wicket.

"Hello."

"Congratulations on your new achievements, Doctor Bumpers. I see now you're a matchmaker, as well as match-saver."

"What are you talking about, Hattie?"

"Luke and my mother, that's who." Luke Wheeler turned out to be the name of the Jumping Jehoshaphat chap I had strongly urged them to hire on the spot, and not alone for the reassuring ring of his expletives. "Those two."

"I don't understand."

"I can't explain over the telephone, but we're in a pool of blood here for real now. You'd better come right out."

"I'm afraid I'm booked up this afternoon," I lied.

"But this is urgent, and can only be handled by seeing for yourself, close up. I couldn't possibly get him in to your office."

"Well, I may have a cancellation in the middle of the afternoon."

I hung up and walked back. "Somebody sick?" a man wearing an indeterminate number of sweaters asked as I went by. "Not yet," I said.

The immediate upshot of the interruption was that the waitress's attitude had visibly softened toward me as the result of some not inconsiderable show of status in the call, no doubt. Women are irresistibly impressed by any trace of the big-shot element. She even told me when she would be through, four o'clock, and would like to, yes, have a drink, in order that we might renew our skirmish under more congenial circumstances. I promised to pick her up then, paid the check without leaving a tip (a rather fine punctilio of taste I thought), and then, deciding to get what must be done over with as soon as possible, headed out toward the farm. On the way, I mentally reviewed the latest chapter in a case I simply could not seem to close, drop, resolve, or otherwise disburden myself of. It was like trying to shake a sheet of flypaper off your fingers.

⊙⊙⊙

Things had started out so well with Luke Wheeler. More than merely auspicious. Taken with him at very first blush, as I say, we had whisked him straight out to Pretty Pass for a working lunch. The latest issue of *Successful Farming* sticking up out of his hind pocket, he had climbed into the back seat with Hattie. We were in Mrs. Sigafoos's station wagon. He offered a steady flow of liberal and informed comments about the surrounding countryside. Of a corn-field being planted just then, he said, "He ain't plowin' near deep enough, I can see that from here. I been plowin' nine inches down lately — a good three inches more'n I used to. Helps build a deeper root-bed and breaks up any compacted plow-sole layers. Plow deeper an' do less tillage, that's it."

Climbing out at the Browns', he cast an equally critical eye around the farm.

"When do you fertilize, ma'am?"

"Spring, generally. We should be getting to it."

"I like to put on most of my fertilizer before I fall-plow. What do you use? I mean most of the land around here is probably pretty high in phosphate."

"That's what the soil tests show. So we've been shifting our fertilizer budget to a little more nitrogen and potash."

He nodded, rubbing his chin. "I reckon what you should

plow down here, more'n likely, is probably, oh, forty-five pounds of nitrogen, a hundred and fifteen pounds of P_2O_5, and, say, a hundred and fifty pounds of K_2O per acre. Varies by field, o' course, but sometimes I also add up to a hundred and ninety pounds of N as anhydrous ammonia."

He sauntered over closer to the field as the rest of us nudged one another with joy, scarcely able to believe our luck.

"Don't know when you had this soil tested last, but I jenny put in thirty to forty pounds more nitrogen just to make sure it ain't limitin', *and* also treat alkali spots in my fields with some additional lagniappe of potassium. Mother Earth likes that." He turned and looked at Hattie sharply. "How many bushels per acre you been gettin', ma'am?"

"Not much over a hundred, I'm afraid. It's been let slide."

He shook his head. "With good hybrids you should net a hundred forty, fifty and even up to sixty bushels per A. Well, it's time to get crackin'. While you ladies fix that lunch you insist on, I'll just poke around the place and see what we got in the way of equipment."

As though this were not enough, we were to be given even more ecstatic reassurance around the luncheon table. He offered to say grace, an auspicious way for a hired hand to make his debut. We all folded our hands and closed our eyes as he plunged in.

"Lord, we are thankful in advance for what we are about to receive, especially seeing as how it comes from the bounty of the land itself. Which we aim to show our appreciation of by cultivating it as conscientious as we know how, and in this way." Here the prayer became a preview of what might be expected of him, no doubt by way of further impressing his employers before salary terms were discussed, but that seemed a petty niggle in view of our find!

"We have the cutworm, wireworm, white grub, root-worm (hope it ain't resistant yet hereabouts), corn root aphid and the rest of the everlasting soil insect complex thou in thy inscrutable wisdom hast seen fit to place here. Well, we aim to use aldrin — oops, that's been took off the market as toxic to humans, ain't it — well then we'll use heptachlor on corn following some other crop (no idea what the rotation's been here yet). On corn following corn, Bux. Bless these unto our use, oh, Lord." He paused to clear his throat. "As to herbicides, this season we'll more'n likely use combinations of Lasso, AAtrex and Ramrod. Bless these also unto our endeavors, that they may prosper in all weathers. Weather. Remember we're gettin' this crop planted late through no fault of our own — the last week in April would have been my choice, but now it'll have to be May. That means the weather will have to be especially ideal; however I guess the corn'll stand a month of cool, wet weather, but pray no more. The yield is going to be down already. But now we must get the corn planted. With thy help, and that 100-horse-power tractor we see out there, the planter, and the 32-foot field cultivator, we hope to realize our aim: get that corn in in five days, mebbe six at the most. But we'll respect our heritage of bounty. We won't run that soil into the ground. Amen."

"Amen!" we all chorused, in our infinite gratitude for this Gift sent from the heaven just addressed.

And now here he was a mere few months later, refusing to clean out the henhouse, like a maid with her no-laundry

proviso. That was only one of the complaints the waiting
Hattie poured out to me on my arrival at the farm. It was
hindsight, but I should have known. It had all been too
perfect, from the agricultural periodical in his back pocket
to the letter-perfect spiels about what should be done. To
say nothing of the way these had been punctuated, now
that I recalled, with pithy asides of a kind that could be all
too swiftly retooled into the style of discourse already making a shambles of Pretty Pass. Besides the mot for heaven's
benefit and ours about not running the soil into the ground,
there had been something about the state Beef Commis-
sion, when that subject had come up. "Beef is somethin'
they *do* more'n help raise, 'ppears to me." Also the way he
had eyed both women, either of whom would have done,
'ppeared to me.

"See what you can do with him about the chicken coop,"
Hattie said, as she led the way to the barn where the
twenty-four-hour wonder was having his lunch break. "It's
a messy job everyone hates, but it's got to be done once a
year."

"Where is Heck?"

"Day for his Spanish lesson. Some of the bunch are wing-
ing down to Guacamole."

Should I as her marriage counselor point out, as dis-
creetly as possible, that guacamole was something you *ate*
in Mexico, not the name of a city you zoomed down to for a
spot of holiday? Or was that outside my province? It was
so hard to know. But it was a clear example of why her
marital relations remained sticky despite all I could do.
Every advance she herself made in getting with it was
automatically cancelled out by some equivalent progress of

147

Heck's own, so that he was always a step ahead of her, in apparently hopeless perpetuation of the gulf between them. She must obviously quicken the rate of her own sophistication if it was ever to become a match for his, and so stabilize the union. Perhaps I was professionally delinquent in letting the moment pass without corrective comment, such as advising her to listen more closely to the place names dropped by the jet set. In any case, she was too full of the pressing crisis involving her mother and the hired man, whom she had come upon the day before taking their pleasure in the very barn toward which we were now slowly making our way. They had been lunching from a picnic hamper Mrs. Sigafoos had packed and brought, with a bottle of wine from Wheeler's apparently unlocatable cache. The cozy little indoor alfresco, so to speak, had been one about which there could be no misunderstanding according to Hattie, who had been stung to quick reproof.

"Look at you. Together. In the hay."

I could vividly imagine her standing arms akimbo like a milkmaid even while couching her reproaches in the language of the city set; and I could as clearly see Luke, chewing placidly as he answered, "No, not in it — on it. Hay's still in bales you can't be said to be in it, just on it, leastways to my reckoning. Little semantic distinction I beg leave to make."

Having brought her account of all these ominous developments to a whispered close, Hattie turned on her heel and left me at the door of the barn, to beard the nonesuch within and bring him to heel as best I could, man to man. I resented the disciplinary mission with which I had been saddled, as certainly above and beyond the call of professional obligation. But giving my belt a hitch, I strode forward into the gloom.

Perched tailorwise on a bale of the hay about which he had been splitting hairs, his back against another, our jewel, or find, was munching cheese and a heel of sausage, which he washed down with red wine drunk straight from the bottle, each swig followed by a pleasurably exhaled "Ah!" Since the tier of bales he occupied stood well above my eye level, I felt at a disadvantage, as though myself facing a tribunal. He offered the bottle to me with a hospitable enough flourish, after hygienically swiping a palm across its mouth. I declined with a shake of my head.

"It's an amusing little cabernet," he said.

"Why is it amusing?"

"There's a bug in it. Left to its own resources it's a mite humdrum. Well, here's to better living through chemistry."

Averting my gaze brought into view an assortment of agricultural implements — a whiffletree, feed buckets, fragments of a horse harness — all of which now seemed less workaday artifacts than *objets trouvés* destined for incorporation into Opal Kitchener's studio constructions. Perhaps our friend, happily chomping away up there, guessed my thoughts as my camera eye panned the interior. Or perhaps he fancied I was wondering where he stowed his liquor supply — which I was, vaguely, though spying on him was not part of my mission. A Chagall poster hung from one rafter, probably left behind by his predecessor. A pullet squawking in flight from a rooster past the open door brought me back to the purpose of my visit.

I stepped over to confront him as squarely as possible in the circumstances.

"Why won't you clean out the henhouse?"

"Reckon I just don't like chickens. One of the most ridiculous animals in the world, you'll have to admit. The only thing that makes us bear the boredom of chickens is our dependence on chicken."

"It hasn't been cleaned out in ten years," I said, the odor from the structure in question causing me to hit on that figure.

He gestured with the bottle. "Good solid precedent for my own prejudice in the matter. My own private resistance to the idea of a-chippin' and a-raspin' and a-chisellin' away at the decade of frosting on that there particular wedding cake."

I paced a moment, then turned to fix him with a level gaze.

"This used to be a good country. Wholesome. Solid. Decent. All our best regional writers have told us that, our poets, our artists. Grant Wood —"

"Please, not while I'm eating." He gnawed off a piece of the sausage and continued. "But you're wrong in sayin' the old-fashioned virtues are gone. That we're still a neighborly Christian folk was shown by a incident I personally witnessed the other day. Fella come into the grocery store to change a bill without buyin' anything — try that in your fancy East! Won't even give you change so you can ride on a bus where you now have to have the exact coins, I hear tell. Well, anyways, this fella comes in and says to the grocer, 'Can you change an eighteen-dollar bill, neighbor?' 'Why, sure, friend,' says the grocer. 'No problem. How do you want it — two nines or three sixes?' "

"Have you ever punched a clock?"

"Yeah, and it struck right back."

That did it. I had had my bellyful of professional bumpkins, homespun sages and rube wits. This was the last straw. Doubtless the long frustration in getting my own love life off the ground redoubled my exasperation over failure to resolve matters here. Oh, how I longed to be shut of this case! How I yearned to slam the file closed on it forever! That goal seemed to recede further with every attempt to attain it: an apparently endless series of chain reactions. I seemed to be plowing a furrow in water, plowing he says! So it is a Crazy Man we see walk with deliberation to the barn door, lean back against it, close his eyes, and draw a long, deep breath, as though to clear his head with a whang of stableyard.

"Now hear this. I own this farm," I fabricated wildly, little knowing how prophetically I spoke, "and I rather suspect, by God and by Jesus, that you are going to haul ass on over to that there chicken coop and clean out that there particular edifice, right after lunch!"

"My, we're on a short fuse today." However, he was visibly sobered by the outburst, so that, even as I turned on my heel and strode back to the house, I sensed that the order given would be most probably obeyed, however imperfectly and with whatever private disrelish.

Both women were watching from the kitchen window as I made my way in that direction. The curtain was let drop when I marched into view. I tramped loudly up the stairs and into the house.

"I think he's had the law laid down to him, all right enough," I said in a tone of guarded optimism. "Hello, Mrs. Sigafoos. How've you been?"

"My mother would like to talk to you now, Doctor Bumpers. It's time you had an interview."

The mother nodded, signing for me to step into the parlor, there to have a word with me alone. Hattie having again withdrawn, she came right to the point.

"I guess you know there's a little something between Luke and me. It started when I agreed to take him in as a roomer. Don't boil over about that, it's all open and above board. Well, do I have your blessing?"

"I have no doubt he sees a good thing here, and is trying to cozy himself into it. That much is obvious."

"Is that your honest opinion, Doctor Bumpers, as my marriage counselor?"

"Bet your boots and save your socks for Sunday," I said, declining a chair and pacing now this room as thoughts of Claire de Lune and the waitress swirled in my head. Himself he could not save — was that it? "All right, give me a little data then. What's his situation? Financial, marital, if any."

"He's a widower — grass, that is. She was no good."

"That from the horse's mouth I have no doubt."

"With her fancy ways, always wanting to go to dances in a long dress that swept the floor — which was more than she ever did herself." Mrs. Sigafoos sat down, though I didn't yet follow suit. "I'm a few years older than him. Old enough to be getting anxious about one last chance at a meaningful relationship, young enough to have it, I flatter myself. Who knows how long any of us will live? I say that in an optimistic sense, not pessimistic. I mean you yourself said geriatrics is still in its infancy —"

"I very much doubt that I —"

"And when you get into more advanced years, you'll have that much more prospect of even greater longevity. Oh, it won't be all roses with us, but is it ever, with anybody? And if it was, how would you make a living? Luke Wheeler's an individualist, as you can see, sharp's a tack and bright's a dollar. A tongue that can easily start an argument, or could if I didn't refuse to be drawn into one. Like you said, it takes two to tangle."

"Actually I —"

"So it would be a case of give and take — like any marriage you could name. Right?"

"And I have a hunch who'll do the one and who the other."

"What they say about a President can work just as well with a man turned husband — that he'll grow with the office."

"Does he still say grace at mealtimes?" I asked with scathing irony.

"Oh, he's not in the least hidebound about that. You see, he thought we expected it, and wanted to make a good first impression. Like I was just trying to say, we can rise to an occasion, use virtues we never knew we had. Like you yourself remarked, a man should be greater than some of his parts."

I had the same back-to-the-wall sensation as a few minutes ago with the subject himself, but without finding the strength to fight back, now. Instead I sank into a chair, letting my arms hang over its arms, so that my fingertips grazed the rug as, with hooded eyes, I raked the parlor as I had the barn. Everything here was as unreal as there. The mahogany whatnot crammed with peachblow figurines, the

Tiffany table lamp, the fringed shawl beneath it, the horse-hair sofa with its scrollwork back, even the dead or living kinfolk returning my gaze from within their plush frames, none of these were any longer furnishings to make a house a home, but only bits of humoresque that had survived a purge as camp. They weren't even curios any longer in the traditional sense, if that meant their being *things;* they weren't things, but rather images in a long, symbolic dream, part of the continuing phantasmagoria that had included the *trompe-l'œil* in the barn, and that now included me too, if it came to that. Because like these objects I had been drained of identity and become a phantom of myself. I had the most overpowering feeling that I didn't exist: hearing myself garbled back in all this constant Malapropese had finally convinced me that I was a figment of Mrs. Sigafoos's imagination.

"Isn't that what you said?"

"I guess."

I heaved a long, defeated sigh, blowing out my cheeks like the wind deity seen propelling a vessel across amethystine waters in a chromo on the wall on which my stare, undoubtedly as glazed as the peachblow figurines, had come to rest. I swung my arms lightly against the sides of the chair, puffing once more, to help inch the ship across the timeless Mediterranean.

"There are times when I just don't understand you, Doctor Bumpers. Here's something tangible that can be counted among the positive fruits of your ministry among us, something you can take credit for as a viable relationship sprung up between two people you were instrumental in bringing together —"

Mrs. Sigafoos broke off and walked to the window, where she stood peering between the curtains at something outside that had caught her attention. She whistled.

"Well, great day in the morning won't you just look who's come round the mountain driving three white horses. Come here."

I stepped over to join her, holding aside the curtain she had relinquished to make room for me.

A large blue Mercury station wagon had pulled into the yard, and a woman alighted from it whom there could be no mistaking. It was none other than the figure of whom I had caught a fleeting glimpse as she flashed by us in the same station wagon, on my first ride back to town with Mrs. Sigafoos, then later seen closer up while lunching with Artie at Ma Peckinpaugh's. In contrast to Mrs. Sigafoos's rather catty remark on that first occasion, her tone was now one of sheer awe as she confirmed my impression by whispering, "It's Ma Godolphin no less." Then she flew to help receive the regal caller at the gate, toward which Hattie herself was rapidly making her way.

◉◉◉

I had never met a tycoon before. Mother Sigafoos was in mufti, but Ma Godolphin beamed, on introduction, from under the visor of her famed blue bonnet, extending a hand as she acknowledged having "heard a lot about me," as well as recalling me from the restaurant, across whose smoky lunch-hour crowds we had been so acutely aware of one another. She was clearly having a ball as reigning celebrity in this part of the country, and there was no mistaking either the animal energy or emotional zest with which she

155

threw herself into the part. She made no bones about having stopped by once more to gaze out across acreage she openly coveted — the last farm left unacquired in a solid block of arable land her corporation now owned and worked, feeding her product line with its yield.

"Somebody's got to keep those damned Eastern fat cats from gobbling it up," she said. "Damned insurance companies and whatnot tilling the Good Earth from their swivel chairs in the Empire State Building." She turned to Hattie. "You know I've been teasing Heck about getting this final piece fitted into my jigsaw puzzle. Where is he?"

"He's in town having his Spanish lesson, Ma. You going with the bunch down to Mexico this weekend?"

"Good God no. Somebody's got to keep Iowa for the Iowans."

There would be no point in concealing the flattery I had found in her continually darted glances in my direction, as though she were inwardly concerned with their effect on me. She now addressed me directly, her full, fleshy lips parted over gleaming white teeth in a slyly speculative smile.

"Maybe I'm offending our young friend here. You are from the East, aren't you, Doctor Bumpers?"

"Only went to school there. I'm from Muscatine originally, Mrs. Godolphin."

She winced in mock pain, holding up her hands. "Please. Call me Ma."

"If you stop calling me Doctor Bumpers. Anyway, so I guess I'm sort of a hybrid. Like all this corn. Soon to become so much relish, what?"

That made her turn toward Mrs. Sigafoos, who, having

looked on with a kind of timorous pleasure at being in the other's mere presence, now positively shimmered under the attention she was given. Her first sarcasm about Ma Godolphin was thus seen as something to be taken with more than a grain of salt. Ma Godolphin, for her part, had just taken over Ma Hmielsk's line of home-made Polish sausages, to say nothing of Ma Terwilliger's Middle Age Spread, a dietetic cheese-and-meat mixture appealing to weight-conscious cocktail snackers, and was probably feeling especially euphoric. Ma Terwilliger had taken a very risky long-shot chance with her choice of name, and had won. Ma Godolphin had bought the product for that name, as movie magnates will buy a book for its title.

"I understand your corn relish is better than mine, Mrs. Sigafoos. I don't like that. To say nothing of that Bloody Mary Mix they use in all the bars instead of mine. I prefer it myself, I don't mind admitting. When are you going to sell out Land's Sakes Brands?"

"On the thirtieth of some February. When elephants roost in maple trees. When Gloria Vanderbilt stops smiling."

"That'll be the day. Well, any time you find —" Here Ma Godolphin broke off, arrested by the sight of a figure seen emerging from the barn. "Good God, isn't that Luke Wheeler? Luke!"

He seemed startled, then visibly reluctant to join us when she beckoned him over, with the gesture of one accustomed to being deferred to. But he managed to repress his annoyance at having been recognized, even recovering some of the arrogance native to his temperament.

"Well, well, hello, Ma. How are you?"

"I didn't realize you had landed here."

The "landed here," with its synonymous echoes of "wound up here," prepared me for the revelations made in the few minutes of conversation between the two. It fell out that this was one of a succession of farms on which he had worked, for periods rarely longer than a year. A thumbnail sketch of a drifter in fact emerged. Born in Both Feet, Utah, some fifty years ago, he had wandered steadily northeastward, fetching up here in the heart of Iowa. He had hired out on one or two of the farms Ma had owned, or ultimately bought, hence her familiarity with him.

"How are your children?"

He looked in a shifty-eyed manner out across the fruited plain, yet at the same time lounging against the front fender of the station wagon around which we were all clustered, as though he was perfectly at ease, had nothing to hide, et cetera.

"Boy's more trouble than eggs Benedict, but the girl! A joy to her father's heart, and would be to any mother's. Research assistant in a medical laboratory in Iowa City. Doesn't turn up near often enough."

"What about your wife?"

"After about twenty-two years with me, you know, she suddenly decided to split. So — she's obviously schizophrenic. Heh-heh-heh."

"She never seemed to be interested or cut out for farm life, from the little I saw of her. Keener on the city and cultural activities."

"Yes. She's on the building committee for that new Civic Center there's all that to-do about. Usual thing — too extravagant, too many frills."

"I know. Like ceiling murals and friezes everywhere, even the walls of the washrooms. Parallels with the Roman Empire and all that. Emphasis on bathrooms. That's what the doomsters say."

Luke shifted his weight a little against the fender, at the same time folding his arms. "Can't see for the life of me why there shouldn't be friezes in bathrooms. After all they're made for relief."

So this gazebo was bi-lingual. He could talk United States, or he could bandy brittle dialogue with the best of them, shifting gears effortlessly from one to the other depending on whether he had to pull the wool over your eyes or the rug out from under you.

"Did they ever find out who burned that barn down?" Ma Godolphin asked him. "You know, at the Gildersleeve farm."

"Nobody could prove it but everyone knows it was Buford. A murky character at best, with an awful grudge ever since he lost that boundary dispute to Gildersleeve. A born loser, but eaten up with unsatisfied ambitions. To get rich, to be mayor, to be first."

Ma nodded. "I know. From the one time I met him you could tell he was filled with rage. I suppose frustration is what makes anti-social characters, mainly."

"Yeah," Luke answered with a philosophical sigh. "An arsonist is jenny someone who's failed to set the world on fire."

It was time to go. I had dallied long enough, though aware of the wealth of new data I had collected in doing so. I said my goodbyes for now all around, and sped back to town, eager to ponder what I had learned — and to keep my cocktail date with the waitress. I hoped nothing would be added to my own rapidly swelling fund of frustrations.

⊚⊚⊚

Vera Mills mellowed swiftly over a few drinks, chatting easily and without militancy about her plans. Her college education had been interrupted after the sophomore year by the need to supplement what her parents could afford with money earned on her own. She could now return in the fall and resume the studies she hoped would make her a credit to her cause — in what direction she didn't know. Perhaps journalism, perhaps some more academic sort of activity. But polemic it must be, of a kind aimed principally, or at least in part, in recruiting male sympathy for the feminist movement. Hence now her apologies for having come out of her corner fighting. An equivalent softening of her face under the dim light in our corner of the cocktail lounge quickened my pulse. The "fast idle" became a racing motor as one envisioned a whirlwind courtship and early, open, marriage. Free association took one at breakneck speed over years lived in rational harmony, each complementing the other in fond respect for one another's profession, always in terms of the separate-but-equal principle to which one would give more than lip service.

The mental engine was still throbbing as one handed her into one's car, closed the door and sprang in beside her and conveyed her to her door. That chivalry would persist through the years: the husband always nimbly enacting the reverse as well, that is, running around to open the door for his wife to get out of the car, the ritual never flagging, never mechanical, but ever expressing the instinctive quix-otic male deference no amount of egalitarian doctrine could deny or dim or expunge.

"Well, this has been delightful," I said as we coasted to a stop before the small white cottage she must still for the nonce call home. "Maybe we can have dinner sometime?"

"Oh, I'd like that. A girl would be keen for that after working on her feet all day as a counterperson."

"Yes."

"By the way, there's a panel discussion at the university next week sponsored by NOW."

"?"

"National Organization of Women. I don't know whether you're interested, but we rotate chairpeople and it's my turn."

"I'll ring you up about that, maybe."

"Because we're serious about this sexual cease-fire. We truly *want* men to dig what we do and what we mean. The vista we want to open isn't for females as against males, or any of that, but for all personkind."

"Yes, well, it's been nice," I said, reaching across her to open the door so she could get out. "Swell we could have the drink together, and I'll probably see you around at the diner anyway."

"Goodbye then."

"Goodbye."

"You have my number."

"I certainly have."

◉◉◉

I reached my office in time to sit glumly there in the gathering dusk. I sighed heavily as I put my feet up on the desk, tilting back in my swivel chair to light up a cigar. I was more than ever depressed about my sexual life, about the seeming absence, anywhere on the horizon, of what I should not myself boggle at calling a meaningful relationship. Must I once again call Artie? Was I reduced to orgies? Were the pickings that slim?

The telephone rang.

"Doctor Bumpers?"

"The same."

"This is Ma Godolphin. Remember me?"

"Oh, hello," I said, taking my feet off the desk. "Nice to hear from you so soon. What can I do for you?"

"That's the question. But I would like to see you. Professionally I mean. It's a matter of some urgency I couldn't of course mention this afternoon. How soon do you suppose you could give me a little time?"

I paused, long enough to be again in the gloom consulting a rather virgin expanse of appointment calendar.

"I can manage tomorrow or the next day."

"Tomorrow will be fine. Almost any time in the afternoon."

"Shall we say two o'clock?"

"Right. I'll see you then."

Sitting there in the deepening twilight, I smiled to myself as I recalled Mother Sigafoos's warning about Ma Godolphin, on the ride back to town that day we'd first met. "Not for nothing is she known as the Wicked Witch of the Middle West."

12

"IT'S BECOME A RATHER SERIOUS PROBLEM BETWEEN TED AND me," Ma began, facing me across the desk with those great, engulfing chocolate eyes; have I told you about them? "Small things have led up to it, of the kind that I suppose are par for the course, meaning nothing more than that the honeymoon is over. Which I gather is a relief to some people, but anyway. You probably hear it all the time. Time was when the husband liked to see his goddess at her ablutions or her toilet. Watch her do her nails or bind up her hair, as she loved to perch on the edge of the tub and watch him shave. My husband even enjoyed the cold creams and other unguents I put on my face and body, in fact found them erotically exciting. You understand what I mean. Lovers do that, you know, use creams like Keri Lotion as an extra sensual pleasure. Slather it on each other and slither around on one another. He would take me in his arms and say it was like making love to greased lightning. Now . . ." She threw out a hand.

"Now?" I gently prompted.

"Now it's, 'Jesus Christ, another lube job? It's like trying to catch the greased pig at a picnic, for Christ's sake. If you need a lube job go to the bloody filling station.' Sometimes ruddy filling station. He's English, you know."

"Godolphin is an esteemed name. Not without its aristocracy, if memory serves. Please go on."

"But these are only the standard little irritations of living together. The sudden discovery by a man that his goddess isn't quite that, or can't manage to go on being that without a regular lube job, to say nothing of a face lift."

I nodded, my fingertips bouncing lightly off of one another. "There is bound to be some disillusionment in marriage."

"Right. But those are the small things. 'Why don't you go to the service station, shall I drive you there to get your bleeding oil changed?' Or it might be just the other way around. The next morning she wants to kiss and make up, and he says no, you make up first and then we'll kiss. Things like that. You can't win."

"Damned if you do and damned if you don't." I slipped a letter knife carefully under the desk blotter. "What's the biggie?"

Ma Godolphin swivelled the chocolate pastilles off to the right a bit, shifting in her chair. She drew a long breath, that made me think for some reason of a gun being cocked.

"I don't know whether you know, but we've been swingers, over the past several years. Of the specific variety I think you understand. We sometimes even wear the buttons that identify, or declare, you as such."

"I understand. You —" I was about to use the term wife-swapping, but a sudden thought of Vera Mills made me bridle at a designation replete with the sense of woman as a chattel, so I changed it in time to mate-swapping.

"Yes. That went on all right for a while, but now . . ." She drew another long breath. "Now he suddenly suspects me of being unfaithful to him."

I looked blankly across the desk a moment, hoping some dawning comprehension about what I thought I'd just heard might spare me the admission that I was at a loss. It didn't, and so I said, "I don't understand. You say you've both been sleeping around, and now you talk about his suspecting you of infidelity. Will you kindly parse that?"

It was her turn to stare blankly at me. She was surprised, shocked even, that I didn't know the morality of the swingers. "You do it in pairs. Couples cross-swapping by mutual agreement. Always. You would never dream of cheating on one another."

"Ah, I see."

Grasping on the instant this particular piece in the mosaic, I now comprehended the whole mosaic itself. It became immediately clear as everything fell into place. The swingers were the Trotskyites in the sexual revolution, then, while those espousing total emancipation were the Bolsheviks. Of course. Not that the two sub-groups in the counter-culture were inimical, mightn't, even, mix and mingle and overlap here and there as chance would betide. Simultaneously, the revelation satisfied me on another point that had troubled me in my practice. It answered in the negative the question whether Heck Brown had been sleeping with Ma Godolphin. He was not. He might very well want to, but was held in check by the rigid morality of the swinger debarring such a — well, "bit on the side," as Ted Godolphin's fellow Englishmen would put it.

"I quite see all that," I said. "What I don't quite understand is what you want me to do."

Sitting in the poke bonnet and granny glasses evocative of pioneer probity, Ma Godolphin looked sixty. She now undid the bow at her chin and set the hat by, shaking out a mass of short-cropped brown ringlets. That seemed magically to transform her into a woman of fifty. If that. She removed the specs and stowed them in her bag. Forty-five. The black lace choker that was also part of the rig was freed of the snaps holding it and flung loose, to reveal the creamy throat and chin of a forty-year-old woman in the bloom of her maturity. She did need glasses, though, and so dug out of the bag a pair of rose-tinted goggles of the kind that can confer an air of chic among women who choose to play it that way. This flurry of re-adjustment left a faint hint of perfume in the room. I got up and slid an already open window up as far as it would go.

"I must get an air conditioner in here. But go on."

"It's now reached the point of his checking up on me wherever I go. He may be out in the hall right now, with his ear to the door or his eye at the keyhole. He's become insanely jealous. He pumps the maid about my callers or about my telephone calls. Are any from men, and who. Beulah's been terribly upset about it herself, and threatens to quit if this continues. He's even gone so far as to phone her husband at home, to ask *him* whether she's gossiped about me. With the further result that Mr. Land gets upset and calls *me* about it, so then *he* becomes a man's voice on the phone, overheard by Ted —"

"Hold it. Just a moment. Your maid's name then," I said, knowing I was well into another *déjà vu*, having already heard what I was going to say next, "as I understand it, is Beulah Land?"

"Yes, and she's a jewel I absolutely do not want to lose."

It was now past the point of having your leg pulled, this name business. It was beginning to seem like outright persecution. I nodded and said, "Proceed."

"Now I'll do more. I'll lay it on the line. What we're up against — much as one hates to use so drastic a term, but the time is past for shilly-shallying — is a persecution complex. Nothing less than that now, so let's not shy at the word. My husband is paranoid. I want you to talk to him."

"I'm sorry, Mrs. Godolphin, that is quite out of the question. I'm not a psychiatrist, or even a lay analyst, though obviously I have a strong background in psychology. Have to have. But I couldn't possibly take the case. I would be arrested. Possibly Doctor von Flivver —"

"But as you yourself say, you have some training in the field, and I don't know anybody else in town I can turn to. It isn't a matter of *treating* him, I'm not asking you that. Just to *talk* to him. Just the act of making him see you, of my insisting he do so, would drive home to him the matter of my total innocence. That's all. Please."

I threw out my hands. "All right. I'll see him *as your marriage counselor*, no more. There must be absolutely no assumption or implication on anyone's part that my participation exceeds those bounds. Now, when do you sup-

pose you could get him to come? Would you try for tomorrow? Because I'd like to get us out of these woods as
soon as possible."

◉◉◉

Godolphin was a handsome man in his forties, with seal-
sleek black hair and dark, downward-tilted eyes of a kind
that hinted at Irish in his ancestry. He had a trim figure,
tailored out in a tight-fitting tweed coat. I knew that he
regularly worked out in a nearby gymnasium, a regimen
which would among other things keep him in shape for the
execution of plans held in readiness for anybody he found
messing about with his wife — "hand him his head." Of
that he assured me early on in the interview. Toward
which he also showed hostility. He resented having been
pressured into it. To gain his confidence, I played a long
shot. One that, if it didn't succeed in that aim, might get
me one upside the chops. But instinct told me I had gauged
my caller right.

"I gather you're quite a swordsman yourself," I said with
a smile.

That took a little of the wind out of his sails. He
shrugged and mumbled something, then simpered rather
foolishly between his knees at the floor. Proving again that
being complimented is always a disconcerting experience. I
pressed my advantage.

"It's obviously the importance of sex to yourself that
makes you paranoid about your wife." I used the word
straight out, so we need not waste time mincing a lot of
others. He stiffened at the term, but I went right on.
"These imaginary men you, rather than she, find under her

bed. Can't you see she's innocent of all these charges? Everybody knows she is but you." I smiled with gentle irony. "The husband is the last to know."

"You really think I'm suffering from persecution complex?"

"No, from the reverse — complex persecution. Persecution of oneself by oneself. The most intricate and vexing kind there is. We can make ourselves and others miserable with it. I say 'we' because I'm no stranger to it myself, I hasten to assure you." I told him a few things about how I often gave myself a hard time, and others with me, in a manner that further gained his confidence. So that it wasn't long before he became somewhat more detailed, even detached, about his suspicions, going so far as to name names.

"You know the Browns I understand."

"Heck and Hattie? Yes. They're very close friends of mine. I'm fond of them both."

"Heck has been one of my suspicions."

"That is absolute and utter rubbish, Godolphin. I can give you my professional word on that, along with my strong advice that you find yourself a good psychiatrist with all speed. Someone who can get to the bottom of this persecution streak of yours, give you some insight into it, as we say, with the aim of purging your life of it, to say nothing of the lives of others."

"Well ... maybe ... I'll see." He had quite thawed out by now, and I was about to counsel him as to what referral channels to pursue in the quest for a competent psychiatrist when he said: "Bumpers, I had the damnedest dream last night."

I waved him off with both arms, flying out of my chair.

"No, no, no. I'm not a psychiatrist I tell you. Save it for whomever you do get. There's von Flivver, also Doctor Solomon —"

"Well, all right. But there's no harm in just *telling* it, the way you would to a friend or acquaintance — or a stranger you met in a bar. So we're just having a drink in this bar, O.K.?"

"I suppose there's no harm in that. But you mustn't expect me to interpret it."

"All right. But sit down. It's pretty long. In fact that's the remarkable thing about it. You know those dreams you get once in a while that go on and on in clear sequence, clear and detailed from minute to minute and from beginning to end? It must have taken me hours to dream because it was *about* something that went on all night. They say time is condensed in our sleep, so that we dream in a few seconds what we imagine takes a lot longer, but I doubt that holds here. It was a beaut, as I think you'll agree after you've heard it."

Here he related a dream of the kind we all in fact occasionally have, in which a tightly knit action is experienced in such vivid detail that in recalling the train of events we seem to be telling a story, or summarizing the plot of a drama possessing the unities of space and time.

"It took place at Pretty Pass," he began, lowering his eyes to fish a cigarette from a silver case. He rose after lighting it and began to walk the room in a way that had me swinging every which way in my swivel chair to keep him in view. "The farmer living there wasn't Heck Brown and it wasn't me and it wasn't a combination of us either —

except that it wasn't anything else. I had a sense of identification with him in some way, in the dream I mean."

"People in our dreams are often composites. We telescope identities. Go on."

"Whoever it was, I'll just have to call him the farmer. An old-fashioned stereotype, the folklore hayseed with the beard and suspenders. I even remember he was wearing Congress slippers. It started off with an old-fashioned snowstorm too. The snow had begun in the gloaming, and busily all the night, had been heaping fields and ... how does it go again?"

"Heaping field and highway, with a silence deep and white."

"Well, that night what does the farmer's luscious daughter tell him but that there's a traveling salesman at the door. He's stuck in a snowdrift at the end of their driveway, marooned there, so that he needs a place to sleep. Tie that! So now we have the traveling salesman and the farmer's daughter setup. Except that the traveling salesman isn't your old-time drummer, but a character driving what he calls a mobile boutique. There *is* one around here, you know, so this character is real. Cyril something his name is. Do you happen to know the swish I mean?"

"Yes. I've seen him twittering about at the Here and Now."

"That's the one. He tools around in this mobile boutique selling wares to the ladies. Modern version of the old itinerant peddler. But the farmer doesn't dig any of this, even after he gets a load of him. He's hung up on City Slickers and the Naughty Nineties, you see. 'Traveling salesman, eh?' he says, foxily. 'Well, we'll have to keep a sharp eye on that buster. And I aim to do more'n that.' The farmer told his son and daughter to switch rooms. But meanwhile the farmer's wife, put on the qui vive by the farmer's words, had told them to change *clothes,* each donning the other's for the similar purpose of outsmarting the slicker. So when shortly after midnight the dude stole down the hall from the room they'd put him up in for the night, to what he had been led to believe was the boy's room, it was to find the girl there, in her brother's pajamas. So it now becomes a Shakespearean transvestite mistaken identity muddle, you see. He made overtures, of which he soon realized the mistake, and realizing he'd been outfoxed he retreated to his room to collect his thoughts and work out a counter-plan. He spent a while at his door, holding it open a crack and listening, wearing some rather extraordinary nightgear of his own which he'd slipped out to the mobile boutique to get before retiring.

"All right. It was now one A.M. By this time the farmer had discovered what his wife had done, and to thicken the plot, he once more stole out in his bare feet to his children's rooms and ordered them to switch back to their own beds but to stay dressed as they were. Here it really gets *As-You-Like-It-ish.* He guessed that the traveling salesman had got wind of all the hugger-mugger going on in the house and was at that very moment plotting to outfox him in turn. So to really confuse him, the farmer flagged his wife as she ran down the corridor bent on some dido of her own, hustled her back to their bedroom and made *her* change nightgowns with *him.* Hers was the kind full of laces and ruffles and bows of course, contrasting with the flannel job classically associated with farmers with appetizing daughters up against drummers and dudes that they were stuck with having to put up for the night. So we can see our own dude in question here over at the Here and Now later, can't we, relating the whole episode as his own *Two Gentlemen of Verona* bit, doubled in spades by the hayseed's now switching garb with his squaw, right down to the tasseled nightcap which he instructed her to pull on over her head. It would have split the Bard's own skull to keep it all straight."

Godolphin paused, only long enough to squash out his cigarette in an ashtray.

"One fifteen A.M. 'Why are we doing this part of it?' asks the wife. 'So if he gets fresh with me, thinking it's you, *pow*, right in the kisser. You can't be too careful with these busters. They'll do anything. You got to get up early to fool them,' says he. 'It's almost time *to* get up,' says she.

"Now the switch took only a few minutes, but long enough for the salesman to dope out how matters more or less stood as of then. The farmer and his wife went back to bed, but the former — the farmer — couldn't sleep. The house seemed *too* quiet, somehow. So he got up again, cautiously opened the door and tiptoed down the hall in his bare feet for one more last-minute patrol. The first spot check he made was of the daughter's room, where she was again fast asleep but still in her brother's pajamas. He was about to awaken her and send her off to climb in with her mother while he curled up here in his wife's nightie in hopes of catching the slicker red-handed when he thought he heard a suspicious noise in the closet. Not the snap of a floorboard, not the scurry of a mouse. No. The rustle of something bigger, say a rat, that had just skedaddled into it to hide. He walked slowly over to it, jerked the door open. There was the salesman, sizing the farmer up from head to foot.

" 'Oh, good, you're in drag,' he says, emerging.

" 'That settles it,' the farmer says. 'I've had enough. You're going to sleep in the barn.'

"The salesman protested, it would be cold in there, he would get pneumonia and so on, but the farmer was adamant. He hustled him down the stairs to the kitchen, marvelling at the getup the other had on, of which he'd never seen the beat. A path had already been shovelled the short distance to the barn, and after seeing him bedded down in the hay with blankets and a flashlight, the farmer climbed back into his own bed, sinking into it with a sigh of gratitude.

"But he found sleep as elusive as ever, and after a time he heard another noise. It was the traveling salesman again, standing outside in the passage. 'There's a tramp at the door,' the salesman said.

"It was now three A.M. The farmer was in drag. The wife in his own nightie and cap was rolling over toward him in the feather bed, likewise now wide awake. Do they call that drag too, in the case of women? No matter.

" 'Jumping Jehoshaphat,' the farmer groaned as he rolled out of bed and into his pants, which he had left on a chair, 'a tramp. Is his name Dusty Rhodes?'

" 'No, that's not her name.' Here our bitchy fag mentioned someone famous for her round heels, 'probably on her way home from some heathen bash when her Jag got caught in the snow. Said to be the prettiest piece of puss ever to come down the pike, *if* you like alliteration.'

" 'Well, Judas Priest,' says the farmer. 'If *that* don't beat the dogs a-fightin'.' "

Godolphin stopped both talking and walking, and stood in the center of the room. "Well, that's it. That's when I woke up — at a point when you *wish* you could know what happened next? But how do you like that for a dream?"

I shook my head in stunned admiration. "Words fail me, except for the farmer's. It beats the dogs a-fightin'."

He sat down, and it was now I who prowled the office, inwardly uncertain, if not downright suspicious, about something. I refrained from attempting any analysis of the dream, as I had said I would, but I did have one question. What had aroused my suspicion was the feeling, not that he was falsifying anything, but withholding it. Something in his manner had alerted me when he had been drawing toward the close of his narrative. I hesitated a moment before posing my question, but at length I could not resist it. I played another hunch. I stepped back to my desk and faced him squarely across it.

"Who was the tramp at the door?"

"Ma Godolphin," he whispered, looking down between his feet again.

Our time was now up, and the puzzle was how precisely to conclude a session I was resolved must be our last, however high the fires of my curiosity had been stoked. In the end I pressed into his hand a book on psychology that I had found impressive, that had been well reviewed in the press, and that he might find helpful in coming to grips with himself. Written in a popular vein, it went into the basic personality types of which we all display variations of one kind or another. I knew that many readers had found it illuminating and helpful in working out their problems. At the very least, it would supplement whatever his psychiatrist would eventually tell him. I shook hands with him and wished him the best, regretting, as I did so, that I wasn't a psychiatrist. Maybe I should continue my training and become one?

13

"ANY MORE THERAPY IDEAS, *Doctor* BUMPERS?"

"Now what?"

"It's about Ted. What you've done has made matters worse. In fact it's terribly urgent. Nothing I can discuss over the phone. Can I come right over?"

"Yes, do."

Ma was in mufti when she arrived, very fetching in a dark blue pants suit and powder blue blouse, wearing the tinted horn-rims and topped with a pink pillbox hat, perched at an angle comfortably short of rakish. She sailed in without preliminaries.

"You remember that book you gave him, to help him do a little homework on himself?"

"Yes."

"At one point it gives the classic psychoanalytic explanation of paranoia. You know what that is."

"Of course. Freud was fully convinced that paranoia stems from repressed homosexuality. The psychic mechanism at work is a drastic denial of the tendency, by which the subject conceals a desire for members of his own gender by converting, or reversing, it into a state of seeming hostility between them, thereby burying his secret deep within his subconscious, as well as from the knowledge of society. Society must never know, no more than he himself. So?"

"So now he's chasing every woman in town."

"Ah, I see. To make *that* compensation for his anxiety. Hmm."

"An anxiety you have inspired."

"I?"

"Oh, inadvertently of course. You didn't mean to but you did — by giving him that damned book. It was an unwise choice. I don't think you know beans about paranoia, Doctor Bumpers."

"I do too know beans about it." I now quite had my back up. People were beginning to *look* like Oliver Hardy as they kept repeating it was another fine mess I had gotten them into. "But at least Sigmund Freud might be credited with some smattering of comprehension about it, wouldn't you say? Look, insight isn't just a catchword of a contemporary science. It goes back thousands of years to 'Know thyself,' and 'The unexamined life isn't worth living,' and 'The proper study of mankind,' and all the rest. *Let* what he's read — and that somebody else has told him, not I — give him a few volts of shock. Maybe it'll help straighten him around in the long run — and get us all out of this seemingly endless rigmarole!" I cried, mostly to myself.

"How long? For the moment he's worse loused up than ever, with this precious insight of yours. What he's now worried about isn't that I'm unfaithful, but that his having thought so reflected this seamy side you've managed to get him obsessed with. So now instead of denying he's paranoid, he's afraid that he is."

"Oh, *I* see."

"Instead of 'I'll kill any man I find with my wife,' it's now 'I'll sleep with any woman I damn please even if it means getting shot by her husband.' Oh, when will this vicious circle come to an end? Do you have any idea what it's like living with a man in such a stew? It's like being married to a kettle of boiling water. What are you doing?"

I had risen and plucked my hat from its hook. "I'm giving this case a change of venue — to the Here and Now or some other handy bar. A sign, once and for all, that I am not 'taking it,' have never 'taken it,' and do not intend to be again construed as doing so. Come on, Ma, we both need a drink."

It being well into mid-afternoon, there were few other patrons in the place and none in the cocktail lounge to a snug corner of which we made our way. After a couple of drinks, Ma grew a little more relaxed, and seemed receptive to my assurances that everything would come out all right in the end. I had no real confidence about what course matters would take; I was hoping, rather than hopeful. In any case, I continued firmly to resist any implication that I was being retained to offer what ministration might be necessary. I was a friend hearing her troubles out, holding her hand in a crisis. That the figure of speech was presently given literal transposition was not my fault. In one outburst over how her own physical pleasures had been reduced in proportion to her husband's widened forages in that quarter, she reached across the small table

that separated us, hardly greater than the combined cir-
cumferences of the coasters on which our drinks reposed,
and clutched my fingers in her own.

"Well, so he's broken the code of the swinger we've stuck
to by mutual agreement all these years. I don't see why I
should hold myself to it, do you? Do you?"

"Well, I suppose . . . In view of . . ."

The pressure of her hand on mine became convulsive,
and as she bent her head closer I felt mine swim in a cloud
of whatever she had scented herself with.

"He's going on a tour through the state beginning next
week. Scouting land up for sale. I think the trip will do him
good in more ways than one. Being away, you know, has a
way of making us worry less about what's going on at home
than when we're there. Out of sight out of mind sort of
thing. Parents have the same experience with children. I
remember that when we were out of town at school or
something, my father and mother didn't stew over the fact
that it was midnight and they hadn't heard us come in yet."
Also, I thought to myself, it will enable him to bolster the
now imperative masculine image of himself by taking on,
for a time, the guise of traveling salesman — our first and
primal national folk archetype of the Lady Killer.

"It wouldn't be any good," I said. "I never get personally
involved with clients. It's rule number one."

"I'm not a client any longer, remember? We're just
friends."

☉☉☉

Has the expression "my type" ever made any sense to
you? I have always found it low in validity. Have the

women to whom we have proved combustible anything in common, except that fact? There are those to whom we are naturally more responsive than others; some to whom we might respond more at one time than another, depending on the amount of inflammable material accumulated within us, so to speak. In my case old frustrations and new vexations, pressures from which a man sometimes plainly and simply needs release, combined with sexual starvation of the moment, these made me — to hammer this metaphor into the ground — tinder to the after all physically incendiary Ma Godolphin. And Ma?

I hope to God I never have another affair with a tycoon. Still, it was exhilarating while it lasted, and, in retrospect, instructive. We both learned a lot from it, and about each other. Ma demonstrated again that the sexual drive is often one with the drive for power that motivates hard-hitting business executives. She hurled herself into love-making with a turbulence that more than once reminded me of Muscles Marinière. She was an orgiast, not that orgies as such were her speed. The Pair was It, and there would never have been a question, for example, of her joining anything like the Baredevils. And there was every reason for my going to bed with Ma to keep her from gobbling up Heck Brown in her need, and thus making an even greater mess of matters at Pretty Pass, to say nothing of finally seducing him, Delilah-like, into selling Godolphin Enterprises the last independently owned and operated farm in that area.

She slept in a luxurious eighteenth-century canopy bed whose blue and gold counterpane matched the tasseled silk overhang, as well as the curtains at its head, which we sometimes let fall for the sense of added seclusion in that delicious nest.

"I've had lots of compliments on this bed."

"That I can believe."

Not that we were always in bed. She liked to make love on the rugs, on the grass, on the roof, in the woods, on chairs and tables and other assorted articles of furniture essential to a well-appointed house, in the pool, behind it, anywhere and anyhow slaking the need for variation. She drew me into her net completely, until I found myself sinking into ever more riotous debaucheries. The climax of our affair, which was also the most extreme of the novelties pursued — the variation to end all variations — occurred one night in late July. Ted Godolphin had begun the last leg of a journey that was, now, to take him out of Iowa into an invasion of Nebraska — proof of her parallel lust for empire. She showed me a postcard from him.

The maid was off, and we were lounging naked on the terrace, sipping drinks. A gentle rain began to fall. I rose, assuming we would seek the shelter of the house. But she stayed me with a gesture, smiling.

"Remember the scene in *Lady Chatterley's Lover* where they run out and make love in the storm? Give themselves not only to each other, but to the elements?"

I admitted vaguely recalling the lyric episode.

"Come, then," she said, and, taking my hand, led me running down the lawn.

"We'll get wet."

"And more than wet."

Her mad pantheistic end, whether planned or extemporized, was soon enough clear. After gamboling about in the rain — a poetic enough escalation over the baths we had taken together, splashing about happy as children — we reached the base of a slope in the lawn that led to a stream at the edge of the property. Recent torrential downpours had swollen it to overflowing its banks, which were now veritable quagmires. It was to this she subtly but unremittingly led me. She threw her head back and stretched her arms abroad, like an abandoned woman giving herself to the Night, the rain streaming down her face and pouring in rivulets along her body. Then she took a tentative step into the marshy bank itself. She wriggled her foot with a delicious shudder, watching the mud trickle between her toes. "Come on, it's fun. More fun than just bathing. I mean — let's take a *real* bath."

"No, Ma."

I stood aghast at her now unmistakable plan. She wanted to be ravished in the mud wallow. I resisted, but she seized my hand again and pulled me in along with her. We were soon in up to our ankles, then we sank in halfway up to our knees. Her breathing quickened, and her voice was hoarse as she said: "Defile me."

"I'm not sure I quite . . ."

"Do you know what a woman is *there*, why she's so easily entered? She's the intertidal slime itself, the Beginning carried over billions of years, a souvenir of it still there between her legs. That's what lubricates her for you. What nursed and splashed the first life into existence. Come on, let's make it complete. Let's go back to the Beginning."

My protests seemed unavailing. If you can imagine

someone shrieking in whispers, that was how she hauled me in and pulled me down on top of her, seizing me in her delirious clutch.

"The two-backed beast again," she raved as I plunged into her despite myself. "And what else did Shakespeare say about a woman being all centaur below the waist?" she panted as we thrashed and churned about in the muck, lashing the bog into a kind of stew as we did. "Now you know. And who was it said woman is clay longing to become mire?"

"I'll try to find out," I gasped. Even as I promised to check into it I was swept into literary associations of my own. Her rhapsodies had rung a bell. Something I couldn't quite place. Then I had it. There is a chapter in Thomas Mann's *Joseph in Egypt* in which the incestuous brother-sister parents of Potiphar go on and on about the womb-dark, swamp-and-river-mud, slithery-slimy primordial mother stuff, and all this, what I was hearing and what I remembered from sources of my own, swirled through my mind as I plowed and plowed and plowed my Ma. There were no limits to the degradation into which she wished to sink in her pursuit to its last literal limits of what the French call *la nostalgie pour la boue* — the nostalgia for the mire. Now with hot incessant moans she demanded that I revile her with every name under heaven.

"Call me a bitch!"

"I will no such thing. A gentleman —"

"Call me that, and sow and cow and whore! Call me slattern, slut, trollop, whelp of a she-wolf!"

I may have ranted a few of these, managing somehow to get the words out as we writhed about in the mud, my voice at last strangled in a dying gasp as, her legs coiled like adders around my back, she heaved us into a simultaneous crisis, sucking the marrow from that bone as the quagmire itself threatened to suck us under in turn.

Our spasms spent, we lay motionless a moment, recovering ourselves. Then slowly I withdrew from her and we both rose to our feet. It was only now that we noticed the rain had stopped. We stood there dripping, every inch of us coated black. Our panting subsided at last. She let fall the hand with which I had pulled her upright. She looked toward the house. She said: "Would you like to freshen up?"

◎◉◎

It was already as we started, slowly, up the incline of the lawn that I sensed, rather than heard, something faintly amiss. The feeling was confirmed by a slight noise from the direction of the terrace for which we were bound, like the scrape of a chair, perhaps. The terrace was illuminated only by lamplight falling from the house, but in it I picked out a figure moving dimly about, now in, now out of, the enshrouding shadows.

My first clear sight of Ted Godolphin is to be forever engraved on my memory for the expression on his face as he caught sight of *us*. He must certainly have thought of us as the "things" that "rise up out of the swamps" in stories told by people who report such ghostly visitations to the newspapers. But after a moment he recognized plainly enough what he had clapped his eye on. I myself was weak with horror as I remembered what he had threatened to do with any man he found with his wife. "Hand him his head" had been his graphic expression. It was my moment of truth. Looking at its brightest possible side, I would in decapitation survive as a sort of Sleepy Hollow legend in these parts, a tale with which to put children to sleep, or beguile an evening around the old campfire. I expected fully to be beaten to a pulp then and there, bleeding from every feature as I spat teeth in all directions — until I saw that he had a hand in his coat pocket. I was to be shot with a pistol, then. At least that would be quicker. Ma was the first to recover from the astonishment in which we were all equally gripped.

"I thought you were in Nebraska, Ted. What in the world are you doing here? Why didn't you telephone me or something that you were coming?"

The answers to these questions seemed perfectly obvious to me, to whose fears of elimination, speedily or by progressive mayhem, were added regrets over the poor judgement I had shown despite my determination not to indulge in the follies all too common in my profession. That there is indeed the school of therapy countenancing, even recommending, sexual relations between patient and psychiatrist under some conditions hardly excused me. I had betrayed my calling. I was not only a quack. I was a quack *manqué*.

The culmination of the scene was not to be much longer delayed. Godolphin stepped down off the terrace onto the grass, and then moved along the house to a point where the light from it brought him into clearer view. I may be mistaken in recalling that his two hands were clasped into a fist, of the kind we make in an attitude of prayerful gratitude. Such a gesture would in any case have been appropriate to the words that now poured out of him.

"So you are unfaithful. I wasn't imagining things," he

said. "You are having an affair, you are cheating on me, thank God! I'm not paranoid after all! It's all true what I've said, it wasn't my imagination, I wasn't imagining things! I'm not crazy, I'm not paranoid, thank God, thank God, I'm not paranoid!"

14

SO THAT WAS HOW I FINALLY SOLVED THE GODOLPHIN CASE. I
was certainly glad to have been instrumental in its resolu-
tion, all the more so because of benefits accruing to the
Browns and their farm. The episode was a kind of shock
treatment, you see, violently restoring balance of a kind
that was as much as the Godolphins could hope for, given
such intricately orchestrated individuals. Reconciliation
between them included the agreement that they would
return to the swingers' pattern of life, from which they had
digressed with such untoward results, and to both. Henceforth neither would cheat on the other, and that barred any
liaisons on Ma's part, including involvements with Heck
Brown such as might further rock the boat at the farm.
Where, of course, the life-style as established must be regarded as permanent. That implies an ever-changing series
of combinations, each of which must be played by ear.
Charlie Achorn returns once in a way, alone, or to coincide
with Cousin Clem or some newcomer to be accorded op-
portunity at the colony; anyone who thinks he might fit in

with a pattern to be henceforth regarded as basic to Pretty Pass.

Cousin Clem goes from strength to strength. He now has an entourage himself: an unfrocked railroad conductor whose familiarities with the female passengers had proved too much even for the Transport Workers Union, who declined to strike when he was given the sack; an out-of-work maid who briefly tried to steal Clem's thunder by applying his methods to music and drama criticism; a sometime sanatarium inmate who thinks he is all four Marx Brothers; and a Lesbian who does Cagney imitations. Dinner invitations to Clem are assumed to include the entourage, though entourages are generally fed in the kitchen, in keeping with custom prevailing there. I might refer to his entourages, in the plural, because there are signs of another cluster of satellites forming, so that he will eventually have two, designating which will attend him on a given evening or to a particular function, the A Group or the B. Sometimes, accosted for an autograph, it amuses him to charge a fee, like Norman Douglas in the restaurants of Capri. When he is not in the mood at all, the retinue serves as a Praetorian Guard protecting him from bores.

It looks as though Mrs. Sigafoos is indeed going to marry Luke Wheeler in the end. There, too, I may pride myself on having been of some help, both in participating in his discovery and unmasking him for the lout that he is. Had I not put my foot down about the chicken coop business, he would not have emerged from the barn when he did in order to attend to it, and so crossed paths with Ma Godolphin, with the resultant disclosures about his two children and so on. Mrs. Sigafoos was thus spared having to find everything out *after* they were married, which would have been far more unsettling than having it all laid out beforehand so that she might go into things with her eyes wide open. You would like to chase him clear back to Both Feet, Utah, but we all know we must give even the worst of us a second chance — often several times over.

It was shortly after these various married lives were set back on an even keel that my own was destined to begin.

⊚⊚⊚

Work and other pressures had prevented my seeing much of Artie Pringle of late, but now that relationship was resumed with a bang, one that was to prove definitive for me. I phoned him about lunch one day, and he said he was booked up for a week with prima donnas on tour, but had something far more colorful to propose.

"How would you like to go to a black mass?" he asked.

"You mean you actually worship the Devil?"

"You got it, Jack."

I hesitated. "Well, I'm not of a very devout nature, I'm afraid."

"Well, that's it. You invert piety into its opposite, and at the same time intensify an emotion you can't any longer have straight. What Genêt preaches as the *good* of evil. It's at Mrs. Renaldi's next Sunday afternoon, after which the Baredevils are mixing it up. It'll be a real wing-ding, I can promise you that."

I went out of a natural curiosity, of course. I was late for the service, slipping as unobtrusively as possible into the last pew when the mass was well in progress. Pew being the last of three rows of chairs lined up at the end of Mrs.

Renaldi's very long living room. I drew a few glares, not for my tardiness as such but because they'd had to start one short of the prescribed thirteen as a result; a full complement now, at least, realized. A priest in a chasuble of firehouse red officiated at an altar contrived out of a naked woman, lying on her back while the priest bent over her, manipulating his materials from her more suggestive quarters. Two choirboys lighted scarlet candles while another presided over an incense pot in which smoldered leaves of henbane and nightshade mingled with acrid resins and asphalt, odors dear to our master, Satan. Anti-fragrances they might have been called. The priest began the litany.

"Prince of Darkness, Administrator of sumptuous sins and all manner of rapturous transgressions, Thee we adore. Thee we worship now and through all eternity. Mainstay of our flesh, Thou givest us all the carnal joys and multifold blisses against which we are adjured by Christianity — that false religion! Only Thee do we serve, that we may through Thy hellish intervention and most diabolical collaboration drink to the dregs — this Cup!" Here he held aloft a chalice symbolic, in this case presumably, of the pagan "cup that cheers," while containing the Devil's personal essence. The satisfactions of the flesh as against the pieties of the spirit celebrated by the Church. Now the blasphemous switch — taking the body and blood of the Prince of Darkness.

Here we were all expected to kneel while the priest passed among us, serving each the profane eucharist. A woman glanced over when I boggled at this, remaining seated in my chair. So I knelt too, not wanting to be a wet blanket again. Since I didn't believe in transubstantiation anyway, I didn't see what harm it could do (though later I did have a little acid indigestion, with some heartburn). I was curious about what they would use for the host. It struck me as something suspiciously like Ritz crackers, while the wine was a paltry little beggar from the Napa Valley country. Personally, it seemed to me that Ritz crackers used in a *regular* mass would have been a lot more sacrilegious.

The communicants having all partaken, the priest, for a sock finish, began to intone a parody of the Apostles' Creed. "I believe in Satan the father almighty, and in Lucifer his —" This was a little rough for me, and so I furtively plugged my ears with my fingers till he was finished, giggling nervously at one point. As with bowed head I also watched with upraised eyes in order to see when the priest was through, I tried to remember who it was said that Baudelaire wasn't an unbeliever at all, merely least of the faithful. Some critic. Baudelaire was Catholic, of course. I suppose none of this is relevant. Just woolgathering.

"— and lust everlasting. Amen," the priest concluded.

All this had been enacted in semi-darkness. Now as we rose the lights swooped on, enabling me to take my bearings. As the congregation moved out through some french windows onto a terrace nearly as big as Mrs. Renaldi's parlor, I looked about to see whether there was anybody I knew. The congregation was roughly divided between men and women. I recognized no one, until Artie came over. I had never been here before; he had simply given me the address and said it would be O.K. just to mention his name to whatever servant accosted me at the door.

"How do you think it went?" he asked.

"I thought it went quite well, on the whole. What happens now?"

"Cocktails, buffet supper later. We'll see how it plays. These evenings at Mrs. Renaldi's are never structured. We wing it. Come on, let's have a drink. The punch here is terrific. It looks like a nice night. We won't be rained out, as we first thought."

Most of the group left, to be replaced in time by an altogether different contingent of guests, so I realized those arriving now were coming solely for the orgy. I kept a nervous eye out for Muscles. There was no sign of her yet. But I presently got a shock of quite another kind.

Shall I say that my heart rose or sank at the sight, on the broad lawn, of Claire de Lune, chatting, drink-in-hand, in a shaft of gold from the setting sun? Let's say my pulse jumped while my spirit plummeted. What in God's name was she doing here? Or I for that matter (though I couldn't repress a secret smile at what the evildoers would have thought if they'd got a load of Ma and me in the pigsty).

"What on earth is Claire doing here?" I asked Artie.

"Oh, the whole thing with her boy friend blew up, and in her disillusionment she figures what the hell. She's going to take the vow tonight."

"Vow?"

"What we call the initiation. Into the Baredevils. You know."

"That undressing on the springboard for all to watch?"

"Yes. Stick around for the show. I'll see you later."

"Does she still work for you?"

"No. She quit."

I withdrew to the far edge of the grounds, half concealing myself beside a clump of bushes in order to watch Claire and collect my thoughts. People soon began to respond to their drinks. One could sense the rioters tuning up. Artie, who had far too light a head for the stuff, was heard spouting poetry, Emily Dickinson of all things. "Inebriate of air am I," he declaimed, flourishing a bottle, "debauchee of dew." The night's real profanation, I thought.

People were getting into their bathing suits and gathering around the pool. I hadn't brought one. No lights were turned on except for a few strings of Japanese lanterns, and so the departed sun had left us to our romantic twilight. Freshening my whiskey, I heard a voice at my side.

"Well, if it isn't Vanilla."

"Hello, Muscles. Long time."

"I've got a bone to pick with you. Something you said to me last time."

So it appeared we were to have a return match after all — and a grudge fight at that. Going two falls out of three with Muscles it was called. I was really not orgy material. I had been clearly wanting in the previous do, I could see in retrospect. I remembered a concatenation called a sextet, into which I'd been instructed to incorporate myself. "Isn't this a trifle baroque?" I'd protested as I mounted from the back the quadruped assigned me. "I'll look it up and let you know," she'd returned over her shoulder. "Come *on*."

Muscles and I were separated by the guests now crowding toward the pool, above which Claire could be seen stepping slowly out to the edge of the diving board. The rule was that a woman stripped from a fully clothed state, not merely shucking off a bathing suit and then hopping in. Claire was wearing a silver dress with long matching gloves, and silver slippers.

As she peeled off the first of the gloves a floodlight suddenly illuminated the scene. A shout went up from the onlookers, one or another of whom caught the gloves and slippers as she threw or kicked them about. I stood at the opposite end of the pool, well back from the crowd, but even from there I thought I could see her blush. She'd had a few drinks to fortify herself, but even so it was an obvious ordeal, because she suddenly abandoned the strip-tease act the ceremony was expected to conform to, hastily unzipping her gown and pulling it over her head. A poolside satyr caught that just short of the water. She wore no stockings, and now stood on the very edge of the springboard looking very pale and fragile and vulnerable in her two remaining silks. As she reached her hands behind her to unhook the brassiere, she caught sight of me standing there. Or so I thought. She hesitated a moment, smiling tremulously. That was when I turned and walked around to the back of the house. I had again reached the shrubbery when I heard an ecstatic outcry, like a long, collective exhalation, punctuated with a whistle or two, and then a loud splash.

I got myself another drink from the bar, a cellarette on wheels that had been trundled onto the terrace, and waited about five minutes. Then I prowled back in the direction of the pool, running smack into her as I rounded a corner of the house. She was in a bathing suit now, rubbing herself briskly with a big towel.

"Bill Bumpers! I thought I saw you out there."

"I thought you thought you did."

"You didn't like my act?"

"I had better things in mind."

"Such as?"

"A drink with you, alone. You know — *really* intimate? Look, go grab that table why don't you," I said, pointing to one only large enough for two, away from the poolside jollifications and out of range of the Japanese lanterns to which the lights had now again been reduced. She named her poison and it wasn't two minutes before we were sitting together, warily sizing one another up as best we could in the shadows.

"When do these bashes explode?" she asked.

"Nothing like that. They just build as everything is played by ear. Improvise with this one or that, see what gives."

"You've been to them before. This is my first, and frankly I wish my mother was here to guide me."

"I aim to function in that role. You were miserable walking that plank. My heart bled for you. It isn't your speed, all this." I edged my chair closer around toward hers. She began to shiver a little under the towel in which she'd draped herself. "And you've ruined it for me."

"How do you mean?" she asked, eyeing me over her drink, which she held cupped in both hands. "Tell me about orgies."

"Well, the trouble with orgies is that if there happens to be someone there you really like, it puts you in an awkward position."

"Are you the club wit?"

"Only unintentionally. I never know what I'm saying. I'll rephrase that."

"No need to. I get your point. Why do you say that though? Is there somebody here who'd embarrass you in that way? Or maybe what you mean is make you self-conscious? A sticky situation?"

"You know it."

"Well . . ." she said, looking away.

"That's not all that makes me uneasy. I've seen men ogling you with an eye to wondering whether you mightn't make a splash of another kind, and I don't like that very much either. In fact . . ." I moved my hand along the table-top till our fingers touched, sending an electric thrill through every nerve. I felt my loins grow weak. Every man knows the experience that can only be described as the most piercing sense of a woman's sheer animal purity. She needn't be pretty to excite it, and this one was. When I bent my head toward hers, her very words were fragrant.

"You've heard I'm on the rebound. An easy take."

"That's a suspicion I could only spike by asking you to marry me. But this isn't the time or place. Did you come with anybody?"

"Not really. Somebody gave me a lift is all."

"Get back into your dress and meet me behind the ga-rage. Or snatch your clothes and come as you are. I'll be waiting."

She threw a sort of quick wild look around, as though casing the prospects for such an escape. She shook her head, in a fit of doubt rather than in the negative. "I'd be a copout . . . ?"

"Look, we already have," I said, my voice dropping to a whisper. "You know that anything goes, at an orgy. Anything. With anybody. I'm not going to use the term gang bang to frighten our little gazelle away. But anything does go — except for one thing. There's one thing you simply don't do at an orgy."

"What's that?"

"Hold hands. My car's the blue Chevy convertible near the road."

15

SO OUR REVELS NOW WERE ENDED, WHILE HAVING ALSO, OF course, only just begun. I don't suppose any of us will ever set the clock so far back as to postpone indulgences until the honeymoon. Still, ours was all a honeymoon could be expected to be. It was what Artie Pringle would have called unstructured. There were no fixed plans to dally on this or that Caribbean island for such and such a length of time. We just winged it, sailing by car through the Wisconsin and Michigan lake countries dear to both our hearts for the common childhood vacation memories they held. Our parents had had resort cottages on lakes near the same Wisconsin city, Fond du Lac. Well, there was a time limit. My schedule was growing tighter as my clients grew in number — referrals from doctors increasing as my reputation in those parts advanced — but I had managed to carve out a solid month of holiday.

Our lives were themselves roughly plotted out. I would continue practicing in Middle City, where Claire could try her wings as an actress in a theatre established there in connection with the local university. A good one, even by the high standards now prevailing for regional academic drama. On my thirtieth birthday I had come into some family money, which I decided to invest in the farm as a mortgage, taken over from one held by the bank. A brief threat of foreclosure sent Heck back to his knitting there, and so it is financially stabilized for some years at least. The setup now enables me to put on a little pressure, whenever needed, and the yield is good. Marriage there continues as a sort of liberal experiment, along the general lines of the institution's having, like the oak tree, to bend in order that it does not break.

The day before our departure I thought I would make a little swing through the old town, beginning with the spot associated with Charlie Achorn. But there was no sign of the homespun sages at the supermarket. Instead I found them lounging on the porch of a grain and feed store called the Oat Cuisine.

"I mind the time I was having drinks at the Algonquin with Thurber," Achorn was telling his cronies. "As we were talking of this, that and the other, some terribly chic couple stopped by for his autograph, and to remark that on a recent European vacation they had read some translations of his work into French. 'And you know,' the woman says, 'I think it's even better that way.' 'Yeah,' says Thurber, 'it loses something in the original.'"

Then out for a quick last look-in at Pretty Pass, where the Browns were paying back everybody and his brother with a cocktail party that was in full swing when I got there.

"I hear Conquistador won another blue ribbon at the hog show, Seth."

"Yes, there's no living with him now, especially if you're a sow. A real male chauvinist pig. I understand you took a flyer in pork belly futures. Did you take a bath?"

"No, no. Broke even. But it's one of those things there's no real percentage in. Like finding your wife under the mistletoe. Speaking of wives, I have a bed date with mine. Has anyone seen her?"

"A while ago, with Sam. Looked to me like she was making last-minute changes in the script."

"She's been wanting to test-drive Sam for a long time. How about you, Lucille? Are you free tonight by any chance?"

"Actually I'm engaged to be married next week. But let's keep it on the back burner."

"Well, grind me into salami and call me a phallic symbol if it ain't Ted Cobleigh. Informed sources tell me you've been to Yugoslavia, Ted."

"For my sins. By car we did it yet. I'll tell you something about the roads in Yugoslavia. They're lower in tar than most cigarettes. When do you go to Jamaica, Prudence?"

"Soon as the maid gets back from Martinique. Inez, I understand your daughter is going great guns at N.Y.U."

"Yes, went there for their Film Department, of course. One of the best in the country. She's been going with a director who's absolutely guaranteed her a job as a script girl on his next picture. It's all very exciting. I mean this sense of being in the cultural thick of it, for our time. Because make no mistake about it, the cinema is the art form of the future."

"I couldn't agree with you more. That's why take my advice and do what Caleb and I are."

"What's that?"

"Put every acre you've got into popcorn."

⊙⊙⊙

Then a dash back to town for an art opening, and a possible farewell glimpse of Cousin Clem in action. I wasn't disappointed. He put his head in the gallery door long enough to get a look at what hung on the walls and remark, "Visual doggerel," before darting on up the street, the A Group at his heels.

I couldn't help noticing a newcomer among them. Lafe Lowry always wore a red cardigan with an open-throated shirt, and a ball player's cap with the bill switched any which way, often clear around to the back. There was generally a quid of tobacco in one cheek, which it was said he could eat lunch without dislodging. He exemplified some sort of lateral mobility as, having flunked out of the shirt-sleeve philosophers, he set out to crash the Clem coterie. At first laughed at by the regulars as a hanger-on hardly occupying the periphery of the B Group, he had steadily sidled and wheeled his way into favor by craftily playing the stooge. He was in good form tonight. There were so many galleries springing up in the general art boom that we had only to cut diagonally across the street to the next show. Here Lafe managed to stay close at Clem's elbow as he made the rounds, somewhat more conscientiously this time.

"Well, whatcha think?" he asked at last. "Idol of them new abstractionists, they say."

"More'n a mite reminiscent."

"Just what do you mean, Clem?"

"Idol's got feet of Klee."

Then around the corner to catch a new fantasist so obvious in *his* derivations that Clem saw fit to lead the entire troupe in a circle of the showroom singing at the tops of their voices "Hello, Dali, well hello, Dali, it's nice to have you back again! . . ."

My work here was finished — and my bride and me could be off on our holiday with a comfortable sense of matters stabilized back home. Our first day's objective was Fond du Lac. That meant an early start and a hard drive. As we neared a mid-point town where we had decided to stop for lunch, we were delayed by a traffic line accumulating behind a small house which was being moved from one place to another. It seemed a cottage of the lake-side resort type with which we were both familiar, vacation snuggeries with names like Bide-a-Wee, Shady Nook and the like. The driver of the flat truck pulling it slowly along periodically drew to the side to let motorists by, and as we shot past it in our turn I glanced over my shoulder to get a look at it. It did, indeed, have one of those name shingles over the front door: Done Roamin'.

After a quick lunch at a restaurant on the Main Street we set out once more on our journey, again encountering Done Roamin' a mile or so out of town. In this case, the jam was soon relieved as the cabin turned off the highway onto a dirt back road, no doubt headed for whatever lake it was being removed to. Its name was so symbolic of what we felt to be our own condition that, as we spurted past it on the high road leading ahead, we waved to it, as though in hopes it would come at last to a happy resting place beside whatever plashing pine-clad shore it was destined for.

203

The nuptial night was all that could be expected, complete with the champagne ritual, for which we managed to get a decent bottle in the hotel where we'd had reservations. By midnight Claire had grown drowsy, and took the "Do Not Disturb" sign off the doorknob and lay down with it on her breast, folding her arms under it.

"Tell me about your first, Mr. Experience."

"You mean my first, well, time?"

"No, no. Your first love. I want to know all about you, from the very beginning, and I shall be able to tell when you're lying, holding back, or exaggerating. You already know too much about me, and that's not a good disadvantage to be starting life out with. So start your odyssey from the beginning. Tell me about your first love."

If the past is prologue, then the epilogue might be something instructively pointing us back to the start. I think every life is a palindrome, which can be read either backward or forward. Of course it may not make any more *sense* than a palindrome, but that is another matter, and beyond the pretensions of this poor chronicle. My wife turned out to be a sort of Scheherazade in reverse, who liked to be told a bedtime story rather than detain you with one, every night. In any case, I wasn't very far into my tale when I knew she wouldn't be awake to hear the end of it. But the reader may find it of interest by way of a nostalgic farewell, and the beginning, or end, of The Palindrome of Billy Bumpers.

◉◉◉

That flaming designation, First Love, then, evokes in my case a picture of a twelve-year-old Muscatine lad riding past the cottage of one Greta Vermeer on his new bicycle. No hands, it goes without saying, if not actually steering with the feet. Proof that one had been suitably seen, from a curtained window or the sidewalk on which one is performing his death-defying feats, was the signal to tool nonchalantly off, perhaps not without a parting flourish: that of rearing up on the hind wheel, momentarily conferring resemblance to a general in an equestrian park statue.

In time one learned the death-defying trick of pedalling backward, that is, switched around on the mount oneself, like the cap on one's head (and Lafe Lowry's in years to come). Naturally I showed off to any girl in sight, but never with anything like the breakneck derring-do with which I rode that bike in Greta Vermeer's neighborhood.

She was a beauty. In coloring orange, with black trim. A de luxe model Ranger, a brand no longer manufactured, but to a Midwestern boy in those days his absolute and quenchless heart's desire, one he would not rest till he possessed. I earned mine with a newspaper route long plied on foot, plucking the papers from a sack slung on my shoulder, rolling them into cylindrical shape, and pitching them at the houses I hurried past. They often landed (in keeping with folklore) on porch roofs or in the shrubbery, so that locating them became what one customer called a treasure hunt — a sour codger who invited me to scrounge in like manner for my fifty-cent Christmas tip. I found it at last, glad to add it to the arduously accumulated savings with which, blessed day, I was finally able to buy the prize, long adored in the window of a sporting goods store.

She (to use again the gender imputed by sailors and motorists to their respective crafts, and by farmers cursing out their agricultural machinery) was a job for which the old word "snazzy" will do. Long rakish lines, a fine spotlight fixed to the frame between her gleaming antlers, and a toolkit that wasn't your leather pouch dangling from the seat but a tapered metal compartment fitted into a double crosspiece running between back and front. It was on this perch that Miss Vermeer, a blue-eyed blonde my own age, sat at last side-saddle, one evening in early autumn as, having picked her up for the purpose and got her hoisted aboard, I wobbled away toward catechism class.

Not mine, hers. The Vermeers were one of many Dutch families scattered throughout Iowa and forming the innumerable Reformed congregations there. As I puffed along the lamplit sidewalk under falling leaves I brushed Greta up on the evening's lesson, which I had managed superficially to cram myself.

"What three things are necessary for thee that thou mayest live and die happily?" I asked.

"First, how great are my sins and miseries," she gave answer. "Second, how I may be . . . let's see . . ."

"Delivered."

"Delivered from my sins and miseries. And third . . ."

"How I may express my gratitude to God for this deliverance, I think," I panted in her ear.

I remember acutely still her fragrant closeness, her hair fluttering against my cheek, the sound of her voice that made my very skin tingle — without in the least exciting those lusts of the flesh she was speeding to hear deplored. Because for all that early love is the most intense we shall ever know, the most obsessive, the most inflaming to the imagination, that sweet fever is chaste. Completely. At that age, we are sick for glimpses of girls we have no real drive even to kiss. Later, we shall want to kiss some girl and do, but not to possess her. And at last we shall want to possess someone and do, possibly unscrupulously, having by that time lost what the Reverend Evelyn Waugh makes no bones about calling our "nursery morality" — virtue and wisdom being, so far from attainments on which we may congratulate ourselves, "the last coin of a legacy that dwindles with time."

So at twelve we can hardly foresee ourselves at twenty-five raving in a motel room about the pagan dignity of mating; but at thirty-five, and I suppose at fifty- and sixty-five, we can most luminously remember the crystal purity of twelve. Intellects who make a profession of explaining to us what we are about tell us that romantic love, classically so-called, is an idealization of the desired sexual object generated by a delay in its possession. A sort of exquisite botheration. But it seems rather that, at some stage of the game at least, idealization is instinctive, waiting on nothing.

Having hung around in front of the church for catechism to be dismissed, I took my damsel home by a roundabout way, to prolong the pleasure of her company. So that before we knew it we were grievously past the curfew hour absolutely fixed by her father, a stern Calvinist who was also an elder in the congregation. Therefore I was pedalling hell-for-leather over the thickened carpet of fallen leaves when danger of another sort suddenly loomed ahead of us.

The town drunk was draped around a lamp-post in a manner leaving no doubt that he had greatly refreshed himself at a neighborhood watering hole. This citizen was quite a sight. Baudelaire has a charming prose poem on the subject of the thyrsus, the ancient staff wreathed with vine leaves that was borne by votaries of Bacchus in their revels. It symbolizes to Baudelaire the counterbalancing opposites of life: the staff typifying will, fixity, support, discipline; the entwining leaves and flowers, freedom, spontaneity, the Dionysian principle. Well, I have never seen anything more thyrsical than that drunk twined about his supporting pillar, Dionysian principle indeed, "spiral paying court to straight line" as ever the poet could have wished. I didn't think of him in those terms then, of course, being as yet innocent of such writers, but I often remembered it years later when, having reached the profane-love stage, I should be reading *Flowers of Evil* aloud to young women in hopes of enlarging their susceptibilities. The scene itself is branded on my memory because of what happened now.

The thyrsus was suddenly dismantled as the drunk disengaged himself from the lamp-post, and the next thing I knew my spotlight picked him out weaving straight into our path, wearing the simper common to tosspots bent on scraping up acquaintance. It was too late to jam on the brakes — something that would have produced a result hardly better than what did occur. To avoid him, I swerved sharply to the left and struck the lamp-post head-on, spilling me and my charge to the ground.

"Oh, my God," I thought from the gutter into which we were dumped, "is she hurt?" And knelt apprehensively over — the bike.

For I have been at no pains to throw dust in your eyes as to what came first in my affections. The whole thing was the principle of chivalry, you see. A boy is going to prefer his bicycle to his girl as the knight did his horse to his lady, to whom he cannot be "errant" save by galloping off, right? Would I ever again gallop off on my steed? Anxiety was far from groundless. Her front tire was blown out like a toy balloon, and the wheel was badly bent, some of the spokes twisted. The frame was even out of line. She would probably be all right, but the damage was serious. I was as wrenched as my mount.

Greta was unharmed, hardly even dishevelled. I could see that at a glance as she came toward me exclaiming, "You're hurt!"

So at least one came last, oneself. One didn't matter. Because I wasn't even aware of the cut on my cheek, bleeding badly, until Greta pulled the handkerchief from my breast pocket and began to dab my wounds. "Oh, it's nothing," I said, untheatrically enough. I trust all this somewhat redresses the perhaps regrettable priority of reflexes in my behavior.

The drunk went mumbling off, feeling no pain, and we continued on in the other direction, wheeling the wounded bike between us, to Greta's house. Nor did I merely bid her good night at the door and scram. I went valiantly inside to brave the wrath of Mr. Vermeer, long enough to take to myself full blame for the lateness of the hour and the gross violation of curfew. Then I walked my lame charger home, for another tender inspection. A couple of weeks in the repair shop known as Mr. Brewer's Bicycle Hospital and we would ride again.

◎◎◎

Is the automobile, in a country where we own cars possessing five times the horse power needed for rational locomotion, a sex symbol? So we are constantly told. In any case, I was soon enough using one to pilot my girls around, including Greta. For years lost sight of, she came into my orbit again shortly after our graduation from different colleges. One Saturday afternoon in midsummer we drove out for a picnic in the woods, spreading our blanket on a river bank. She had fixed a hamper of goodies to which I contributed a couple of bottles of wine. The weather was idyllic. She stretched out on the grass, after our feast, flinging her arms wide with a long sigh of pleasure, and gazed lazily up through a maple tree beneath which we had settled ourselves.

"It's perfect," she said. "Paradise."

Perhaps not for long. I drew from my coat pocket a volume of verse calculated to signal the end of innocence.

"Are you going to read me some poetry, Bill?"

"Why not?"

"Who?"

"How about some Baudelaire?"

Overhead the serpent could be seen, twined, thyrsus-like, among the boughs of the gently rustling maple tree.

⊚⊚⊚

Well, I had known I should be telling half the story to myself. I took the "Do Not Disturb" sign off the sleeping bride and hung it on the hotel room door, managing to do so, and then slip into bed beside her, without waking her up.

I lay wide-eyed myself. Directly beneath the open window of our second-story room was a maple tree whose boughs overspread a nearby street-lamp, so there was a constant play of shadow on the ceiling as a faint night breeze gently stirred them. Sight of it prolonged the memory on which I had just touched, as though I were looking at the negative of a cherished snapshot. Why should it so haunt me now? Greta had married early, and been soon divorced. That was all I'd heard in the intervening years. What had happened to her since then? What was happening to her now? This very minute? Maybe she'd needed me — not that I quite knew in what sense I meant that. Plans for the return journey home from Wisconsin included a brief stopover at Muscatine. I might make inquiries there ... ask ... and just possibly even ...

I found the thought of all this vaguely disturbing as, my hands laced under my head, I gazed upward at the sinuous play of the maple boughs on the ceiling above, so that I was a long time in finally falling asleep, and that only after I'd got up and drawn the window-shade all the way down.